This is a work of fiction. Names, characters, businesses, places, events, locales and incidents are either the products of the author's imagination or used in a fictitious manner. Any resemblance to actual persons, living or dead, or actual events is purely coincidental.

For Lucille and Paul, my biggest supporters

"Maui no ka oi"

Right next to the endlessly roaring Pacific waves lies the
old wind-beaten house. Surrounded by tall swaying palm
trees, giant wooded plumerias, hibiscus and poinsettias that
always seem to be in bloom and fill the air with their strong
scent. Set to the side are some old macadamia nut and other
fruit trees and the remains of a vegetable garden and some
neglected scraggly pineapple plants. There is an old
weathered stone wall around the property, but it was really
never needed since visitors were always welcome and there
was nobody to be kept out. The house could use a new coat
of paint, but it looks just charming the way it is with its
grayish-blue antique patina. It's quite a stately two-story,
one family home, built in the 50's or 60's, bigger than all
of the rather smallish surrounding houses, with three bedrooms and an open loft-style living-room with an entire
glass front facing the ocean. These glass windows can be
turned open like blinds to lure the breezy trade winds into
the house. On very rough days, when the wild ocean mist
almost sprays up to the house, you can feel the salt on your
skin even inside the house. A wraparound porch encases the
entire back of the building & we have to think of the parties
or quiet romantic hours that must have taken place here in
the day. Past the yard, leading down to the ocean, is black
volcanic rock, rugged and abrasive, just the way it must have
flown into the ocean millions of years ago and then cooled
off while hitting the water. An old forgotten wooden swing,
tied to a strong tree branch, sways gently in the wind and
makes us think of a dreamy child, sitting here for hours,
hypnotized by the waves and the beautiful ocean view.
In the distance, out in the wild ocean, we can see the
greenish-black rocks of Alau Island, appearing out of
nowhere like a shark's fin. If we turn the other way and
look southeast, we can see the far right side of the sea
cliffs surrounding Hamoa Beach, the beautiful
crescent shaped beach which James Michener called
the most beautiful beach in the Pacific. There is also
a small detached guesthouse, connected to the main
house by a bamboo covered breezeway.

Chapter 1
Rhinebeck, Hudson Valley

Lani Winters, a beautiful vibrant young woman in her late twenties with Polynesian features, was just returning from a long walk through the dreary cold February weather in Rhinebeck in the Hudson Valley with her two stout Basset Hounds, Lucy and Lilly. The sun was just rising and a few early birds had just started chirping in the leafless branches of the bare trees. She was walking with dragging feet and was not her usual cheery self. She had slept poorly… actually, she hadn't slept at all… the past few nights and it seemed that her eyes were in a constant state of being red and puffy from crying. Her boyfriend of almost six years, Michael, had told her a few days ago that he had met someone else, packed his bags and left. The worst thing about the break up was that they had started their plant nursery business together and now he wanted her to buy him out, since she was the one who would keep their mutual plant nursery and flower shop. Michael's new girlfriend had a dance studio in New York City and he had no more interest in staying in the Hudson Valley. The nursery had not been doing well and was more in the red than in the black, and Lani didn't know how she would ever have enough money to buy him out.

She opened the mailbox to check the mail as she stepped into the driveway leading to her flower/gift shop and in the back to three green-houses belonging to the nursery. Piles of letters fell toward her as she opened the front latch, and she tried to catch them before they fell onto the muddy ground. Apparently, the mail had been stacking up since she hadn't checked it in days…

"Gosh, again nothing but bills!" Lani said out loud, to no one in particular. "Bills, bills, nothing but bills! If this keeps up like this, I'll have to sell the nursery or file for bankruptcy and Michael can see where he gets his money from."

She was at her wits' end. The nursery had done really well for a few years since they had started it, but ever since a chain hardware store with an attached nursery had opened a branch a few miles down the road, lots of customers stayed away, buying quantity instead of quality, and the business had started struggling. Especially in the winter, when they had to pay horrendous power bills to keep the greenhouses heated. That might have been one of the reasons that Michael was over the relationship and owning a nursery. They had to let an employee go, and life had become all work and no play and they were so tired in the evenings they would fall asleep in front of the TV and had started behaving like an old couple with life having no more excitement to offer. Michael had started going to his favorite bar instead, didn't come home until early in the morning and then would be too hungover the next day to be of any use to anyone.

With a disgusted face, Lani picked some muddied letters up that had fallen on the ground with her finger tips, while the two Bassets both pulled into different directions on their double leash – one around the mailbox the one way, the second the other way. They almost made her fall while she was struggling to not drop all of the letters into the mud again.

"Girls!" she shouted. "You're making me fall!" And of course she stepped into a puddle right in front of the mailbox. She dropped the leash so that they would get stuck on the mailbox and would just have to stop walking. Lani quickly opened the carabiner of Lilly's leash, unwrapped it from the mailbox and snapped it back on and of course ended up getting her hands muddy. But if she didn't, the Bassets might catch some scent and would be gone faster than she could blink. They walked past the flower shop, which was in the front, to a side entrance leading into her modest house, and she tossed the pile of letters onto the other piles of paperwork and mail on the kitchen counter that made it look rather messy.

Lani looked from the messy counter over to an easel with a half completed painting of a beautiful orchid, which has been standing in her live-in kitchen for quite a while now. She rolled her eyes. If only she could ever complete something. She was always so busy that she never had time for anything else…

Someone knocked urgently at the door and she was distracted yet again. The dogs ran to the door, barking, but wagging their tails and whimpering at the same time. Who would stop by this early, Lani thought to herself.

"Hang on a second! I'm coming!" she shouted as she rushed to the front door, while she glanced in the mirror in the hallway and straightened her messy ponytail a little with one hand.

She pulled the door open carefully, while she tried to hold the dogs back and now stood face to face with her neighbor Bill Vanders, who also happened to own a nursery, specializing in shrubs and landscape plants. His nursery still seemed to be doing OK, despite the new chain home improvement store, since he also was a landscape architect and did more upscale landscape projects for businesses in the city. Bill was the only one who was happy that Lani and Michael had broken up, because he had always had a not-so-secret crush on her and was hoping to fill the empty space in Lani's heart.

"Good morning, Lani. You look great, as usual. Hey, girls!" He kneeled down to pet Lilly and Lucy who were excited to see him and could obviously smell the scent of his dog on him. Bill's face beamed with excitement. He always looked for a reason to stop by and see Lani, and today he had a good excuse.

"The mailman mistakenly left this letter in my mailbox. It's for you and it seems important. Looks like it's from a lawyer. I'm surprised they didn't send it Certified mail…"

He handed her a letter with some fancy tropical stamps on it from a law firm. She took the letter and thanked him, but didn't really pay attention to it, because she was more concerned about getting rid of Bill who had already stepped from the foyer into the kitchen and was working hard to try and strike up a conversation. She liked him, but just as a friend, and a new relationship was the last thing she wanted. It was going to take her a while to get over Michael.

"I really had a rough night. Bessy heard some animals again and barked all night. I could really use a cup of coffee..." Bill hinted, looking longingly at the coffee maker. Even though there was plenty of time before she had to open the flower shop at 9AM, she tried to find an excuse to get rid of him.

"Ummm, I really have to water the plants and do some accounting before I open the store. You know how it is to be so busy..." she replied.

"Oh, come on, one coffee, I have to tell you about McGill's nursery. They've filed for bankruptcy."

This was an area with lots of nurseries and Lani's wasn't the only one that was having difficulties. One after the other was closing due to the stiff competition. Lani held her breath for a second. She was next if some wonder didn't happen...

"I'll make you a coffee to go," she offered. "I'm really running late today... Please tell me about McGill's another time..."

"Okay, that's great. How about dinner later in the week? We could also talk about the merger between our nurseries that I've been wanting to propose..."

Since times were tough for smaller specialized nurseries in general, Bill had the idea to form a co-op of nurseries to make them more competitive with the bigger chains. Of course, this would also be another excuse to spend more time with Lani...

"Ummm..." she hesitated, searching for a way out. "Sorry, you know my mom had knee surgery and I really have to help my parents out this week."

"Oh ... OK, maybe next week?" Bill said, wistfully. "How's your mom feeling?"

"She's okay, but she can't get much work done... I'll let you know about next week," she replied, as she made for the doorway to hopefully lead Bill back out.

"And I also really wanted to tell you how sorry I am about you and Michael," Bill lied.

"Thanks. Just wasn't meant to be, I guess…" she replied. "Thank you so much for bringing the letter over, but I really have to go now. Bye!" she said, as she ushered him out, pretending that she was in a rush.

She actually did walk into the front greenhouse, where she immediately got distracted again, looking at some beautiful orchids and other flowers with buds that were starting to open. She took some pictures with her phone and posted them on her flower shop's social media page. When she was in the greenhouses, she was so in her element that she forgot about the world around her and any worries she had.

Just a few minutes before nine, she realized how late it was and that she had to open the flower shop in a few minutes. She rushed back to the house, took a quick shower, put some clean clothes on, poured herself a coffee, grabbed a banana and left for the flower shop. She had already forgotten about the lawyer's letter…

Her phone started ringing while she was walking into the store.

"Hello?" she listened. It was Lani's mother, Lynn Winters. "Oh, good morning, Mom! How are you feeling?"

"Great, honey, thanks for asking. I just wanted to check in. How did you sleep? Did you eat anything? I'm worried about you."

"Everything's okay, Mom. I'll get over it. Michael and I really didn't get along that well anymore. I'll be over tonight after work and after walking the girls."

"Why don't you bring the girls with you? I'd love to see them."

"Okay, sure, I'll bring them with me. Do you want me to bring some groceries or can Dad go shopping?"

"Thanks, honey. Dad already went shopping and we still have some of the spaghetti and meatballs you made the other day, so we can have leftovers. We can make a salad to stretch it a little," Lynn replied.

"Okay, I'll see you later, I have a customer, Mom, gotta go." Lani ended the call, as her first customer of the day entered the store. It was a regular, one of her mother's local friends, Mrs. Smith, who bought a couple of nice flower bouquets for the reception area and conference room of her law firm once a week. She could have sent someone to pick up her bouquets or have Lani deliver them, but she was into flowers and plants as well and loved to stop by and chat with Lani and look at the new orchids in Lani's collection.

Lani greeted Mrs. Smith cheerfully.

"Hi, Mrs. Smith! How are you today?"

"I'm great! I'm in quite a rush though. No time for the greenhouse today. I'll just grab the bouquets and be gone. I have an important hearing this morning. I'll try to make it over on Sunday, when the Orchid Society comes over!"

She paid and was about to leave the store, but then she turned around and asked Lani:

"I hope you're okay? I heard about Michael."

"I'm not too peachy, but I'll be alright, thanks for asking," replied Lani.

"Chin up, you are going to fall right back on your feet, my dear."

"Thanks, Mrs. Smith."

"Bye. Hang in there."

"Bye."

Lani sighed. She hated being reminded about Michael by everyone, but Rhinebeck was like a small village. Everyone knew everyone and there was always lots of gossip.

As soon as the door had closed behind Mrs. Smith, Anne arrived. She was a young college student who worked for Lani on an hourly basis to help out in the nursery and deliver bouquets to the restaurants and hotels that ordered flowers on a regular basis. Lani handed a tray full of bouquets to Anne. They were wrapped up in special paper to protect them against the cold.

"I'll see you later," said Anne and walked toward the door.

"Please don't forget to take the flowers for my mom to her first. She needs something to cheer her up". Lani smiled. Anne smiled back at Lani, nodded and was gone.

Lani received some phone calls with orders for flower bouquets and had a few more customers, then she finished up some accounting and the long day was finally over. It had been too slow again to cover all the expenses and some work in the greenhouses had to wait, because Lani couldn't handle the tough manual labor all by herself. I might have to hire someone and try to get a loan from the bank or borrow some money from my parents, thought Lani. A bit heavy-hearted, she locked the front door and went back through the store to her living area in the same building. She really liked her profession and didn't want to give up her beloved flower shop and nursery. She had been the one who had pushed to start their own business when she and Michael had met each other, both doing their internships in the Northern Dutchess Botanical Gardens right after college.

As soon as she stepped into the house, the girls came running up happily. Lilly, the older one of the two, had a toy in her mouth that was full of drool, which she offered to Lani.

"Yuck, thanks Lilly! There you are, girls! You are seriously the best anti-depression medication!" She happily hugged them and played with Lilly and the toy for a bit, until the girls started wrestling with each other. Lani let them out into the small fenced backyard and went to change into some workout clothes for their evening walk. During their walk, Lani stopped by at her parents, Lynn and Mark Winters, who lived just up the road, in walking distance from Lani's house. They were the best distraction for Lani and tried to avoid the subject Michael, who had never been their first choice of son-in-laws.

Chapter 2

A few days later, Lani was puttering around in her kitchen, trying to clear off the counter a bit, since her best friends Theresa and Sarah were going to stop by, when she came across the letter that Bill had brought her, which she had totally forgotten about. She stopped in her tracks.

"Wow, what's this? Oh my gosh, I totally forgot about this...", she exclaimed, surprised. "It sure looks exotic..." She read who the sender was:

KAHANANUI & SONS LLC
ATTORNEYS AT LAW
32 LANALILO STREET
KAHULUI, HAWAII 96732

And yes, it was addressed to her, Lani Winters, Rhinebeck, NY. The stamps were beautiful: colorful tropical plants and flowers that made her immediately want to travel to where the letter had originated. Hawaii had always been the place of her dreams (with the emphasis on dreams since it seemed so far away and unattainable...), since she had grown up in the Hudson Valley, but had a Hawaiian name (Lani = sky, royalty) and very obviously seemed to be of Hawaiian descent with her distinct Polynesian features.

She was still staring indecisively at the unopened letter when the doorbell rang. Theresa and Sarah entered, went through the Basset greeting ceremony and then gave their friend Lani lots of hugs to cheer her up.

"He wasn't good enough for you," said Theresa, "Be glad you're rid of him."

"That tramp," said Sarah, "she won't be happy with him either."
Lani smiled a sad smile. She knew they were just trying to make her feel better.

"Whatcha got there?" asked Sarah, as soon as the dogs had settled down under the kitchen table and they had all taken a seat.

"A letter from a lawyer in Hawaii."

"Come on, Lani, open it!" said Sarah. She was so curious that she almost snatched it out of Lani's hand. Before Sarah could grab the letter, Lani got up, walked over to the counter and grabbed a knife that she substituted for a letter opener, neatly slicing the top of the envelope open. She pulled out a folded piece of paper and read... She had to sit down. Her jaw dropped.

While staring at the letter, she explained to her girlfriends: "It's a letter from this lawyer... Pike...," it took her a while to be able to pronounce his last name, "Ka-ha-na-nui, informing me that my great-aunt, Mrs. Malani Kahale, passed away on January 20th and that I'm the sole heir of her estate and I inherited a house... Koki Beach House in Hana, wherever that is.... and there's a date on which Mrs. Kahale's Last Will and Testament will be read in the Kahananui offices in Kahului, and I am requested to be present for that. What the heck? I have never heard of Malani Kahale? And I have to fly to Maui? That's not going to be cheap..."

Sarah and Theresa were speechless for a second. So was Lani. None of the three knew what to say, while they were all still staring at the letter. Then Sarah finally said:

"Let me see!" Lani handed her the letter.
Sarah looked at the letter, the signature at the bottom, *Pike Kahananui, Attorney at Law*, and the law firm's stamp under the signature.

"Well, it sure looks legit." Sarah said and handed it to Theresa.

"Yup, it doesn't look like a joke to me!" exclaimed Theresa. She added jokingly:

"Take us with you, we'll all go and check it out together!"

"Hmmm...that's not a bad idea," replied Lani giggling.

"You should call the lawyer and ask him what's up with this and who this woman is exactly, and how they know that she's your great aunt- and how they even got your name and address. Maybe it's a scam", said Sarah, pointing at the name *Malani Kahale*. "You could probably still call right now. Oh, wait ... it's Saturday!"

Lani was still so shocked about the news, she didn't want to call the lawyer right away anyhow. She wanted to talk to her parents first, show them the letter and let it sink in a little.

"I'll call him on Monday." Lani answered. "Let me digest this first. I think I need a drink!"

She got up, walked over to the fridge and got a bottle of Chardonnay out and grabbed three wine glasses from a shelf and poured the glasses almost up to the brim, still in shock. They all laughed and Sarah and proposed a toast:

"Well, thanks for the great pour! To your new house! May it be a beautiful mansion on some tropical beach!"

"With my luck it's going to be some little shack in the jungle, but you never know," laughed Lani.

They clinked glasses. Lani took a big sip of her wine. She had a strange feeling, but also felt a bit excited. Having been adopted, she had always been curious about finding out who her biological parents were, and this was the first she had ever heard from any family she might have besides her adoptive parents. Since Lynn and Mark had always been the best parents in the world, she had never really felt the urge to search for her biological parents, but this letter did make her curious…

Chapter 3

The next day was Sunday, but still a work day for Lani. It was the busiest day of the week for her and her favorite one. People didn't only stop by to buy flowers, but tourists and locals, sometimes even orchid societies, stopped by just to come and tour the greenhouses to see the orchids and other plants. Lani loved meeting people and talking about some of the things she loved most in the world – orchids and other tropical plants. She had the reputation of having some very rare and beautiful plants in her collection.

She did open up the nursery later on Sundays, so she usually walked over to have breakfast with her parents in the morning, before she started working. Lani was glad to be able to sleep in today, since she had quite a headache from all the wine she, Theresa and Sarah had consumed last night. Lani's friends also hadn't left until 1:30 am, so she didn't mind, during their walk, that the Bassets stopped at every bush and sniffed for what seemed an eternity. She was also very thoughtful because of the letter. She wondered how her parents would react when she told them about it…

The Bassets automatically turned into Lynn and Mark Winters' driveway and pulled Lani behind them.

"Slow down, girls!" Lani could barely hold the dogs and, once again, she felt like she was getting carpal tunnel syndrome from them tugging at the leashes. They knew that some juicy treats were always waiting for them here and they loved Lani's parents.

Mark Winters, a tall slim older man with thick grey hair, wearing a pair of old jeans and a sweater with leather patches on the elbows, was in front of the house, standing on a ladder, replacing the light bulbs in two outside lanterns. He was quite handy and always stayed busy. If it wasn't in his and his wife Lynn's house, it was in his daughter's nursery or somewhere else in town, adding some money to their modest retirement fund as former elementary school teachers.

"Hey there, girls! Hey, Lani! How's your Sunday going so far?" he greeted them cheerfully, quickly climbed down the ladder, gave his daughter a hug and warded off Lilly and Lucy who were jumping up on him and almost knocking him over with their heavy bodies.

"Good. I could use some coffee. Theresa and Sarah came over last night and stayed quite late."

"Come on in, I think Mom has breakfast ready," Mark replied. He was glad that Lani's friends had been over so late and distracted her.

They entered the small, cozy and tastefully furnished house and walked into the big live-in kitchen with a nice tiled stove, the centerpiece of the kitchen, that was not only used for cooking, but also to heat the room. Lani's beautiful flower bouquet was on the table that Lynn had already set for breakfast.

"Hey, Mom! How are you?" said Lani and greeted her mom with a quick peck on the cheek.

Lynn, tall and slender just like her husband, her grey hair pulled back in a knot, dressed in leggings and a cheery colorful, yet tasteful longer sweater, was currently walking on a cane after just going through knee replacement surgery. She was happy to see her daughter and tried kissing her as well, but she got distracted by the two spoiled Bassets demanding her full attention, and she quickly turned around toward the counter to pick up two homemade dog treats, which they snatched out of her hand faster than she could blink.

"Hey, girls! There you go!" Now that the Bassets were busy, she gave Lani a quick hug and finally answered "I'm great, Lani! Thanks again for the beautiful flowers! Have a seat. I'll get you some coffee, and would you like a homemade cinnamon roll?"

Lani answered: "I can get it, Mom! You should be resting…".

"No, I'm fine, my knee is already feeling much better today." She was not a person to complain and sit around. Lynn took a closer look at Lani. "You look tired. I'm sure you haven't been sleeping well. Are you going to be okay?" Lynn knew about Michael, but she could immediately tell that something else was wrong with her daughter. They had a pretty good relationship and were quite close.

"Hmmm…" Lani had wanted to wait for the perfect moment to tell her parents about the letter, but she was never able to keep a secret from them. "Well… I got the strangest letter in the mail yesterday… look." She pulled the letter out of her pocket, took it out of the envelope and put it on the table.

Lani's parents' faces turned pale and they looked at each other when they saw the letter's sender. Lani definitely had roots in Hawaii, but that was basically all they knew. They had adopted Lani at a time when they lived in California, and when a baby from the Hawaiian Islands was offered to them by the adoption agency, they had happily welcomed her, but of course the entire adoption process had remained anonymous. Her heritage was all they ever found out, and of course her Polynesian features were very distinctive. But the name Pike Kahananui did ring a bell to Lani's parents and they felt bad that they had never told her about him. Ever since they had adopted Lani, this same law firm had sent them a monthly check from an anonymous donor who wanted to contribute and help with Lani's upbringing until Lani was 18. It was not a significant amount, but they had never had to touch it and, because of that, it had added up to quite a sum. They had put the money into a savings fund that they wanted to give her with her inheritance or whenever it was urgently needed. The break up with Michael seemed to be the right time and now there seemed to be two reasons for her to need the money… This might be a good time to tell her about it, they both thought to themselves…

Lani read the letter out loud to them and looked at them, quizzically.

"I know you guys never made a secret of me being adopted, but is there anything else you know about this woman, Malani Kahele?"

Both of Lani's parents shook their heads, they were still too shocked to be able to say anything. They had always been afraid of Lani's "real" family in Hawaii contacting her and that she would go there and they'd "lose" her to those beautiful tropical islands that were so far away.

Lani continued: "Why would a stranger leave me an entire house somewhere in the boonies? I looked up where this Hana is. It's about two hours away from any civilization. You have to drive this really dangerous road along cliffs and through hairpin needle curves to get there. Do you guys think I should even go and look at it or just turn it down?"

Mark and Lynn looked at her with serious faces and then at each other. They had been dreading this moment, but knew they couldn't hold her back. A bird will only come back if you let it fly. It was time for Lani to travel to the place where she was born. They both slowly nodded at each other and then Mark turned toward Lani and said:

"We think you should go. Maybe you'll find some information about your biological parents. Just go and visit."

Lani stared at them. She had mixed feelings about this whole thing. On the one hand, she was curious and had always wondered where she came from, but on the other hand she was upset about a mother or parents who had obviously abandoned her and just given her up for adoption.

They all finished eating their breakfast and drinking their coffee rather thoughtfully and quietly. Lynn and Mark tried to act normal, but glanced insecurely at Lani, who was definitely somewhere else with her thoughts. This was a lot to handle at once.

When Lani stood up, because the Sunday work day was calling, Lynn said quietly: "You have to do what's best for you, darling. Think about it for a day or two. You have until…" she looked at the letter one more time that was still on the table "… oh, you have until…" then she looked up at a calendar by the kitchen door "you have until, oh, wow, Tuesday, to make up your mind. That's not much time they gave you. I wonder how long it took for the letter to get here…"

She picked up the envelope and turned it around, trying to look for a date on the postal stamp.

Lani blushed a bit, but it was a moot point. It didn't matter that the letter had been lying in her kitchen covered by other paperwork for almost an entire week. She had 48 hours to call Pike Kahananui and let him know whether she was coming to the reading of her great-aunt's

Last Will and Testament or not. And that appointment was two weeks later in Kahului, the biggest city on Maui.

Chapter 4

That afternoon, Lani really didn't have too much time to think about the letter, since she had an entire group of orchid enthusiasts, the Mid-Hudson Orchid Society, visiting her nursery.... Until it turned out that one of the newer members, an older lady, was Hawaiian. She involved Lani in a conversation...

"Did you bring any of these wonderful Cattleya from Hawaii?" she asked Lani, automatically assuming that Lani was from Hawaii...

"No, I didn't," answered Lani. "I've actually never been there. My mom or dad must be Hawaiian, but I was adopted."

"You definitely have to go one day. It's magical. Being in Hawaii brings you such a terrific sense of peace and calm. Especially if you have Hawaiian blood, you need to go and find your roots, especially to Maui, but that's just my personal favorite and where I'm from... Maui no ka oi - Maui is the best."

Words that would soon be engraved in Lani's mind. But right now they just made her curious, very curious.

The woman purchased a beautiful big specimen Cattleya that Lani had a hard time parting with, but business was business and she needed the cash. How strange, Lani thought to herself. I've never met a Hawaiian person in my entire life and now, of all times, I run into one who makes me even more curious about going...

The next day, she called the offices of Pike Kahananui and confirmed that she would be coming to the reading of Malani Kahele's Last Will and Testament in two weeks in Kahului. She had about a thousand further questions for Pike Kahananui, but he was not available to talk and the answers would have to wait, if he even had them... She asked the receptionist for his email address to send him a few first questions about the appointment and wrote it down.

She'd be able to scrape up enough money for a flight to Kahului. It wasn't the most expensive season, even though it was never cheap to fly to Hawaii. And it was a 12-hour flight with at least one layover, usually in California. The biggest challenge would be to find someone to take care of the nursery while she was gone and also someone to take care of the dogs. She couldn't just close the business for two weeks, she had a lot of running expenses and, even though the watering system was automated, it still needed to be supervised. The plants and orchids couldn't be left alone for two weeks.

Sarah and Theresa stopped by and they all brainstormed.

"I can take care of the flower shop," said Sarah, "but probably not of your prized orchid collection." She made a cutting motion with her flat hand in front of her neck. "They'd be goners in two days."

"I can help Sarah," exclaimed Theresa.

"Yeah, right," answered Lani. "With your three kids under eight years old and a husband and a dog, you barely have time to take care of yourself! You're not helping with the store! Maybe you and the kids can walk the dogs from time to time, but even that might be a bit hard with the way the girls walk…"

"How about Bill?" hinted Theresa.

"Noooo way!" Lani had also briefly thought of him, because he was a plant expert, but he'd just get his hopes up if she gave him an inch…

"He's the only one of us who knows how to take care of your orchids", said Sarah. "And he's not that bad… he is NICE. I wouldn't kick him out of bed…"

"Yeah, my grandmother is nice too!" Lani laughed. "My mother can also take care of orchids. I just have to see how well she'll do with her knee in two weeks. She might be too busy with rehab. But it's not only the orchids. It's the other plants and greenhouses too. And I really can't have Sarah work in the shop fulltime. It's not like you don't have a life," she said to Sarah.

Sarah was actually what they called "independently wealthy". She managed some rental properties that her father owned, but didn't spend much time in the office. She seemed to spend more time driving around in her nice Porsche, going on dates and hanging out at the mall in nearby Poughkeepsie. Theresa and Lani loved hearing her stories involving her flirts with men, which she told in a rather comical manner.

"It's totally fine," answered Sarah. "I can work on my laptop in your flower shop and answer my phone calls and organize anything that has to be done from there. And if I have an emergency and have to leave, I can just close the store for a little bit, or maybe Anne can help out."

Lani perked her ears. That was an excellent idea. Anne had been asking for more responsibility and she'd be able to work longer hours – it was just the money that made Lani nervous.
She hated asking her parents for money, but she might have to ask them for a small loan.

Well, Lani's parents couldn't stop thinking about Lani's trip to Maui and the money that they had received for 18 years and had been saving for her. They had come over and now knocked at the front door. Lilly and Lucy started baying and crying as if they knew who it was. Lani walked to the front door and opened it carefully to check who was there and not let the dogs out.

"Oh, hey, Mom and Dad! What's going on? Come on in!"
Lani's parents didn't know that Lani's friends were over.

Lynn said shyly "Oh, hey, girls, sorry, we didn't know you were having a little get together. Shall we come back another time?"

"Noooo!" said all three of them at the same time. "You're not bothering us - have a glass of wine." Lani went and got two more glasses of wine, set them down in front of her parents and poured them both a glass. "We're trying to figure out how I can go to Maui and what to do with the nursery and Lilly and Lucy. It's actually good that you stopped by. You could help us brainstorm. I wanted to ask you if you could take the girls. Do you think that would be okay, or is it too much with your knee, Mom?"

"I think I'll be okay in two weeks, I'm starting physical therapy tomorrow, but maybe we can find someone to walk them in the mornings and then drop them back off at our house? Dad won't be available much," she said, looking at Mark. "He is starting a pretty big renovation job next week…"

Ugh, Lani, Sarah and Theresa looked at each other. Mark got these bigger kitchen or bathroom renovation projects from time to time, so he was going to be quite busy… So, Lynn might be overwhelmed with taking care of the orchids…

"No, I think I'll be fine with the orchids, as long as someone takes care of the other greenhouses."

Lani replied: "I was going to ask Anne if she wants to work more hours. I guess I could train her by then, but I'm not sure if I can afford to pay her…"

"Well, that's actually the reason we stopped by," chimed Mark in. "We came to give you something that we've been keeping for an emergency, and we think that emergency is right now. Is it okay that we give this to you while Sarah and Theresa are here?"

"I have no secrets from Sarah and Theresa, you know how close we are, Dad," replied Lani with a smile. "But what's the surprise?"

Mark had an envelope in his hand, which he now handed to Lani in an official manner. Inside was a juicy check from her parents, made out to her.

"Wha… what? Where did this come from?" Lani was quite speechless. She knew they weren't the wealthiest people with their social securities as former elementary school teachers…

Mark replied: "Well, with all these things going on, you and Michael breaking up, a great-aunt who suddenly left you a house and you traveling to Maui, we think it's time for another revelation. The same lawyer who sent you the letter, Pike Kahananui, sent us a monthly check, ever since we adopted you, from an anonymous benefactor who wanted to help us raise you. Until you were 18 years old. Then it stopped. It might have been from the same great-aunt, we have no idea. We never used the money and saved it for you and wanted to give it to you as part of your inheritance. So, that time has come now and it's all yours."

"It might make things easier for your trip to Maui, and you might be able to give Michael some of his money without having to get a loan," added Lynn.

It was quite an emotional moment. All five of them had teary eyes, but Lani was really crying tears of joy. She loved her parents so much. They always did the right thing and saved the day. They had done it again. She jumped up, ran around the table and hugged both of them.

"You guys are so awesome! Thank you! This is a fortune! Now I don't have to worry about the nursery anymore! I can hire Anne fulltime for two weeks and I don't have to worry about where to stay in Maui either! I was afraid I was going to have to camp there!" she said laughing.

They all lifted their glasses and Lynn proposed a toast: "To your trip to Maui, and may you find there what you are hoping for!"

Chapter 5

Lani couldn't sleep that night. She tossed and turned, thinking about some mysterious person, sending her a check month after month for 18 years. Who was this anonymous person? Was it her mother, father or was it her great-aunt? Would she find any other relatives in Maui? Although - she seemed to be the only one if she had inherited the house… then she finally drifted off to sleep, but had nightmares about driving along a really dangerous coastal road to a little shack in the jungle where her parents were sitting on the porch, with spiders crawling all over them, crying and stretching their arms out for her…

She woke up, covered in sweat and had to turn the light on her nightstand on. What a nightmare! She shook herself in disgust about the spiders. She calmed herself down by remembering that spiders were important for the environment and ate mosquitoes and other pests...

She thought about her parents. Despite all the excitement and her travel plans, she felt bad about leaving them. She made sure to stop by their house the next morning while she was walking the dogs. Her parents were excited for her and kept bringing up the trip to Maui. They didn't seem upset. Instead, they seemed happy for her. At least they have each other, thought Lani. Some of her friends only had one parent and it was worse to leave them alone. Mark had gotten some of their old suitcases out of the attic and offered her to use one or two of them.

"This one is perfect!" said Lani. "Thanks a lot, I can really use it. I haven't even thought about packing yet. I'll be super busy training Anne until I leave. But I think I might have to go to the mall in Poughkeepsie and look for a new bathing suit."

"Maybe you can ask Bill to stop by and supervise the equipment in the nursery from time to time. He does know the business."

At first, Lani made a face, but then she thought about the idea. It did make sense. Bill was right next door and was really the only one who knew how the system with the automated sprinklers worked and the heaters too. He had basically taught Lani and Michael everything they knew about running and taking care of a greenhouse.

"Yeah, maybe you're right. I'll talk to him…"
And I'll talk to him about being just friends and not getting his hopes up, she thought to herself.
So, Lani finally called Bill and asked him to have dinner with her.

A few hours later, they were sitting across from each other at the local middle-class steak house "Harry's". Not too casual, but also not very fancy. It was a nice place with a dark wood interior and good steaks. Bill was beaming all over his face again and Lani wasn't sure if she regretted meeting him, because she didn't want to get his hopes up… He was a very nice guy and she really liked him, but not in a romantic way. She needed a break from relationships for a while. I guess I'm going to have to get that out of the way once and for all too, she thought to herself.

They ordered drinks and while they were sitting there silently, looking at their menus, Lani said:

"Ummm… Bill, you kow I really like you, but as a friend. Is there any way we can just be friends? Not in a romantic kind of way? Do you know what I mean? You know, Michael and I were together for quite a while, and it was a tough break up, and I'm really not ready for a new relationship. Sorry, now I'm babbling…"

They both looked at each other and laughed. If Bill was upset or disappointed, he was very good about hiding it.

"Yes, I like you," Bill admitted, "And I wish you felt differently, but I respect that you don't want to go from one relationship to the next. I'm okay with just being friends."

"Thanks." said Lani. She felt as if a big weight had been lifted off of her shoulders. At least things were out in the open now.

The waiter Tom, who was an old friend of theirs, came back to take their orders.

"Ladies first, what would you like, my dear?"

Lani knew exactly what she wanted, since she always ordered the same thing when she was here: "I'll have a New York Strip, medium rare, with a loaded baked potato, please."

Tom nodded. "And what type of salad do you prefer? House or Caesar?"

"House, please, with Italian dressing on the side," answered Lani.

"And how about you, Bill?"

"I'll have the 16 ounce Rib-Eye, medium, also with a loaded baked potato and Caesar Salad."

"Thanks, guys, is there anything else I can bring you right now?"

"Some bread with your famous garlic oil would be great. Thanks, Tom!" answered Bill, then he turned back toward Lani: "So, what do you need help with when you go to Maui? Of course I've heard about your trip. It sounds very exciting. You know, Rhinebeck is a small town. Lots of gossip…"

Lani grinned. She knew everyone was talking about her sudden inheritance and the trip to Maui. The gossipers must be going crazy trying to figure out what was going on.

"I really don't know if this is asking too much, and I know you have your own fulltime job and business you have to take care of … but do you think there's any way you could kind of supervise Anne and my mom while they take care of my nursery together? I mean, just stop by once a day and check if everything's okay? You're really the only one who knows the Dosatron and the other equipment like the heaters. Of course I'd like to pay you…"

"Sure, I can help. But you are not going to pay me. It's not like I'll be working around the clock. It sounds more like I just have to check the greenhouse temperatures and the watering system once a day and be in touch with Anne in case of emergencies. That won't be a big deal. It's just a favor between friends and good Karma for me. Or maybe you'll be able to visit some cool nurseries in Maui and can send me a nice awapuhi ginger plant. Those are so cool."

They smiled at each other. Lani always wondered if men and women could just have a platonic friendship, she would see if this worked out or not... She planned on paying him something anyway or maybe she could really bring or ship a special plant from Maui to him…

The waiter Tom brought their salads and they both started eating with a great appetite.

Chapter 6

Lani's departure date moved closer and closer. She was very busy training Anne and was almost thankful for the fact that the nursery was so slow this time of year. Anne was very smart and picked things up quickly, but it was a lot to learn. Lani even showed her some of the orchid care to possibly give her mom a break. Most of the orchids had a resting period, so that they would only have to be watered about once a week during the time Lani was gone.

The morning of her departure was quite a scene, because, even though Sarah was taking her to the airport, everyone wanted to say goodbye and showed up at her house, which almost turned into a party and made her late. Lynn and Mark came over with a tray of home-made muffins and a goodie bag with snacks for Lani's long flight, Theresa showed up with her youngest daughter Tatiana, Anne was there to get some last instructions and Bill showed up as well to wish Lani a safe trip. The Bassets were mulling about, waddling in between everybody's legs, enjoying the company, but they were a bit nervous and kept a sharp eye on Lani, because they seemed to know what the packed suitcases meant…

Outside, they all said their goodbyes, and Sarah got into the driver's seat of Lani's car and pulled up to the front door. They were driving Lani's car because Sarah's Porsche was too small for luggage. Bill, being a gentleman, took the suitcase and Lani's carry-on and lifted them into the trunk.

"Have a safe trip, Lani," said Lynn "and keep us posted. Please call when you land in Maui," she added as Lani gave her a big hug and a kiss on her cheek.

"Have a great trip, kiddo!" said her father when it was his turn for a hug.

Lani gave him a big kiss on the cheek as well.

"Love you, Dad. I'll call you guys from San Francisco. I have quite a long layover."

"Have a great time, Lani! You know I'm green with envy!" said Theresa, and Lani gave little Tatiana a hug and kiss as well.

"Bye, Bill and thanks for all your help." said Lani and Bill gave her a friendly hug.

"Safe travels and have the time of your life!" he said.

They all waved as the car pulled out of the driveway. Off she was…

Chapter 7

The plane was descending slowly. The landing gear was deployed, as the plane was getting ready to land at Kahului airport. The purser announced:

"Aloha, ladies and gentlemen, in a few minutes we will be landing in Kahului airport. Local time is 6 pm and the temperature is a balmy 84 degrees Fahrenheit. On behalf of Hawaiian Air Travel and the entire crew, I'd like to say "Mahalo" for joining us on this trip and we are looking forward to seeing you on board again in the near future. Have a nice stay in Maui!"

Lani looked out of the window at the home of her mother and her ancestors, saw the West Maui Mountains and dome of Haleakala, which had been formed through at least three series of major volcanic eruptions. The shape of the lava showed us how it must have poured into the water and then suddenly cooled off, hitting the Pacific Ocean, which was now sparkling in all shades of green and blue in the glistening sunshine. The plane touched down and Lani could hear and feel the powerful brakes of the plane, while she sped past tall palm trees swaying in the wind and some hangars belonging to Kahului airport and a few parked smaller planes. Lani was excited. Her heart was pounding in her chest. This trip was so exciting!

She stepped out into the smallish open arrival terminal of Kahului Airport, felt a warm wind in her face, the famous trade winds, but also the balmy warmth which immediately made her take her jacket off. She walked over to baggage claim, where Mr. Pike Kahananui, her great-aunt's lawyer, an older heavyset Hawaiian gentleman, was already waiting for her with a sign that had her name written on it. They shook hands and he put a beautiful yellow colored lei with a heavenly scent around her neck, made of puakenikeni flowers, one of Hawaii's most fragrant flowers. Mr. Kahananui introduced himself with a gentle deep voice and expressed his sincere condolences for the death of her great-aunt. They got into his car and he drove Lani to the car rental location, where they picked up a smaller compact car for her.

She was following his car now and he drove ahead, leaving Kahului behind them and heading toward a nearby town named Paia. There were palm trees on both sides of the road and colorful flowering shrubs as far as her eyes could reach, and the beautiful turquoise colored ocean on the left. He took her to a nice little hotel in Paia, "Paia Bed & Breakfast", and after they had parked their cars, she asked:

"Isn't the meeting tomorrow in Kahului? Why did we come all the way here?"

"Paia is a much nicer area for you to have a nice dinner and walk around and relax a little after your long flight. I also get a special rate at this hotel. You can drive back into Kahului tomorrow morning, you saw for yourself, it's not that far…"

"That's true – I guess you're right!" she replied with a smile, looking around, enchanted by the nice little town with quaint gift shops and restaurants and the ocean right in the back of the one side of the street.

"I'm sorry that I can't have dinner with you. I have an important meeting with another client tonight."

"That's okay. I'll be alright," Lani replied with a smile. She was way too tired for a conversation anyhow and didn't mind being alone. "I'm very thankful that you picked me up and brought me here."

"I will see you tomorrow at 10 am in my office." He shook her hand and was gone.

She was glad to have some time to herself to unpack a few items for tomorrow and then get something to eat. She was tired and hungry after the long flight. Lani went to her room and stepped out onto her own private little patio with nice bamboo furniture. She wanted to take a shower and change into some more summery clothes before she went and grabbed something to eat. She was amazed by the beautiful view. She could look straight out onto the ocean and watched the gigantic waves crash into the sand. Some late surfers were still out there, hanging onto their boards, while they bobbed up and down in the surf, waiting patiently for the next perfect wave. Tall palm trees and tropical foliage surrounded the little patio. The sun was slowly setting, and everything was dipped in beautiful shades of red and pink.

Lani left the hotel and walked up the main street in Paia. Mr. Kahananui had recommended a few places to eat. She walked up a side street and arrived in front of the restaurant that had been Mr. Kahananui's first choice. A casual, but very nice looking fish restaurant. She sat down and a waitress brought her a menu. The menu sounded amazing. Some of the names she didn't even dare pronounce, because she knew the waitress would burst out in laughter. The waitress was very nice and read the types of fish out loud for her.

"Mahi, Ahi Tuna, Ono, Hapu'upu'u, Opakapaka, Kajiki. You will learn how to pronounce them. You look like you're going to be a natural," she said with a grin, meaning Lani's Hawaiian features, not too shy about saying what she thought. "I highly recommend the Ono tonight. It was locally caught today and comes with couscous, a very nice buttery white wine sauce and a medley of locally grown organic veggies."

Lani looked at the menu for another second. "I'll have the Ono, please," answered Lani and smiled back at her. "Thanks."

The food was to die for. Lani already loved Maui. Everything smelled good, everything tasted good and everybody seemed nice and they all seemed to "Live Aloha", which Lani had read meant showing love, affection, compassion, mercy, sympathy, pity, kindness or grace.

After dinner, she walked back down the road toward her hotel, looking through the windows of the stores. Everything was closed now, but people were still milling about, standing in front of ice cream parlors, shave ice stands, restaurants, just hanging out, chit-chatting and enjoying life.

Chapter 8

The next morning, Lani woke up at 5 am by the sound of waves crashing against the shore and she was starving. For the first time in her life, she was suffering from jet lag. It was already 11 am in the Hudson Valley, and her internal clock knew that. She tossed and turned for a while, but then she gave up trying to go back to sleep and threw the sheets back and jumped up, full of energy.

"Well, I guess I'll have enough time to get ready for the appointment at ten", she said to herself with a grin. She pulled a simple t-shirt dress over and walked across the patio, down to the beach.

It was still dark, but there was already a little bit of light on the horizon where the sun was about to rise. The waves crashing against the shore sounded powerful, yet soothing. The sand felt soft and warm between her toes. Lani sat down in the sand, leaned against a palm tree and just watched the ocean, the clouds, the stars and the moon that were slowly fading as the sun slowly crawled up in the sky and night turned to day.

Some surfers came running down the beach with their surfboards, yelling something in a different language, while they pushed their surfboards into the water, laid down on them and started paddling out past the wave break. Lani startled. She had fallen asleep to the soothing sound of the waves! She looked at her phone and realized it was almost 8 am! She couldn't believe it. She must have been pretty tired. Now she actually had to hurry up to get breakfast somewhere and drive back to Kahului. One more glance at the ocean, where some other surfers were already patiently waiting for the perfect wave. Two handsome young men heading to the water with surfboards in hand glanced at Lani and wondered who this beautiful stranger was. Lani turned around and walked back up to her room.

She took a quick shower and walked into the lobby where she realized that the hotel offered a nice breakfast buffet. She had delicious pancakes with coconut syrup, lots of fresh fruit and hot Kona coffee.

What a nice way to start the day! Pike had advised her to check out before the appointment, since she was going to drive to Hana right after their meeting, so she checked out of the hotel, put the lawyer's office into her GPS and made her way back to Kahului.

She arrived at *32 LANALILO STREET*, parked in front of the offices of Kahananui & Sons LLC, Attorneys at Law, and entered the old stately former residence, surrounded by a tropical garden. She was greeted warmly by Pike Kahananui, who led Lani into his handsome office, with beautiful teak wood accents and furniture.

Mr. Kahananui read the Last Will and Testament of Mahali Kahele and confirmed:
Lani Winters was the sole heir of Mahali Kahele's estate. But this appointment didn't give Lani any further information on why Mahali Kahele left her the house or who her biological parents were. Pike Kahananui didn't have any information about them either. He only knew that Lani was Mahali's great niece. He read all the conditions and disclaimers of the inheritance out loud to her. She had the right to accept it or turn it down within nine months. The house was not in very good shape and had to be renovated within one year. If not, it was going to be sold to an investor, who had already provided the law firm with a letter of intent, confirmed availability of funds through his bank and the proceeds would go to an orphanage in Honolulu.
Also, a caretaker, a good friend of the family, Max Palakiko, lived in the guesthouse and had the right to live there at least until the renovation was completed, so that he could supervise and assist with the progress. Lani still had no idea how valuable the house was in such a desirable location two minutes away from famous Hamoa Beach in one of the most expensive locations in the world. She still thought it was some little house out in the jungle and probably not very valuable.
The period she had to either accept or turn down the inheritance would give her time to go and check out the house and see how much work was needed and then see if she could and wanted to come up with the necessary money and decide what to do.

Chapter 9
The Road to Hana

Pike Kahananui and Lani shook hands in front of the office. He had given her the address of Koki Beach House and she was on her way. She was nervous, since she had heard that the Road to Hana could be quite dangerous and treacherous.

"Take your time and enjoy yourself. You might need the whole day to get there and you're not in a rush. The Road to Hana is about the journey and not the destination. If someone is in back of you and you feel rushed, pull over to the side and let him or her pass. Don't let anyone make you go faster than you should and always drive defensively."

Lani nodded.

"You can download an app on your phone and it will tell you where to stop. Grab a sandwich and some water in Paia and have a picnic somewhere. There are also going to be fruit and ice cream stands on the way. Make sure to stop at Pineapple Peter's and say hi to him from me. He is an old friend."

She nodded again, a bit nervous to be going on this adventure on her own, but she had already gotten this far…

"Once you get to Hana, stop at one of the general stores and pick up some groceries for dinner and breakfast. I'm not sure how well Max has stocked the refrigerator in the house. There is also a very good fruit stand on the right once you enter Hana belonging to Maui Farms. You might want to stop there too. Try to get to Hana before dark. You don't want to be driving those curves at night."

Lani looked at the clock on her phone and was now in a hurry to leave.

Pike Kahananui stood on the side of the road, watching Lani depart. He slightly shook his head. We don't know what he was thinking. We weren't sure whether he knew more than he had told Lani or not. Why had Lani been put up for adoption and why did her great-aunt want her to return to Maui now, after her death…?

Lani didn't remain very anxious with the beautiful surroundings she was passing through. It was all quite distracting, although she had to make sure to concentrate on the road. There was quite a lot of traffic. She stopped briefly at a grocery store in Paia to grab some waters and a sandwich and some cut fruit. She also bought a little cooler that she could store everything in. Then she continued to Ho'okipa Lookout where she parked, glanced quickly at the jewelry and fruit stands and watched some surfers out in the beautiful rough ocean, bobbing up and down, waiting for the next wave to ride ashore. She walked down a long driveway heading to the beach and discovered a bunch of Hawaiian Green Sea Turtles, "Honu", resting in the sand. Wow, they must be a majestic sight swimming in the ocean, Lani thought to herself. They were giant, yet beautiful creatures.

She walked back up to her car and continued her drive to Hana. The street didn't seem too bad yet, but then it changed quickly: from time to time she had to slow down in a very sharp curve and watch out for oncoming traffic. Some little bridges were so narrow that she had to wait for the traffic on the other side to pass before she could drive across the bridge. It was definitely white-knuckle driving.

She passed some beautiful Rainbow Eucalyptus trees on the left that looked like out of a fairy tale or as if children had colored their trunks with chalk. What an enchanted place this was. She stopped on the side of the road and walked up to the trees, looking up at their colorful trunks, feeling like in a different world, and she smelled their strong eucalyptus scent in the air.

Lani had to realize that she couldn't stop at every waterfall or outlook, it would take her three days to get to Hana if she did. So, she just enjoyed the slow and steady drive, every time she felt like a car or a bigger van full of tourists was pushing her, she just stopped on the right side of the road and let them pass.

Next she came up to the Garden of Eden Arboretum. She was dying to go inside and walk around, since she was obsessed with plants and this seemed like the place to go. But there was a charge to get in and she knew that it would take her hours to look at everything and enjoy it, so she decided to leave it aside and keep it on her list of things to return to, maybe even for a day trip from Hana.

Some really dangerous hairpin-needle curves and one-lane bridges came up and she had to really watch the road and hold on to the steering wheel. This part was really tricky and she started sweating. She soon came up to a fork in the road. The left paved road lead straight down to the Ke'anae Peninsula. She looked at the car's clock which said 1:00 pm, and her growling stomach and her hands that hurt from grabbing the steering wheel so tightly, also told her that it was time to eat a late lunch, so she took a left down to Keanea. The guide book told her that Keanea was a traditional Hawaiian village and known for its extensive taro fields. She passed a beautiful old stone church and drove out to an area where the wild waves were crashing against the lava rock, parked her car next to some others and walked out onto the harsh black lava field, but had to quickly retreat to not get soaked by the waves, or worse, knocked over by them and pulled into the ocean. She sat down on a little stone wall next to some other people, relaxed for a while and ate her sandwich and the remaining fruit and just watched the waves roll in. She loved the wild rough ocean with the jagged black lava.

She continued her drive and realized how urgently she needed coffee. Jet lag was kicking in again.

First she came up to Pua'a Kaa State Wayside Park, which supposedly offered a quick hike to a waterfall and freshwater pool, as well as bathrooms and a picnic area, so she actually unpacked her bathing suit and took it to the bathroom and changed into it. She was so warm and sweaty that she actually didn't care about not having a towel, she would dry off somehow and figure it out then. Her t-shirt dress was made of terry cloth, so that would help… and a quick dip in a cold pool would wake her up again.

The waterfall was pretty and very refreshing and Lani was almost dry again by the time she was back at the car. She put her terry cloth dress on top of her bikini and wiggled to open it up in the back and pull it out and exchanged her bikini bottom for another dry one in the tight little car, and there she was. Ready to continue her adventure.

Just another few miles and she came up to Pineapple Peter's famous ice cream stand. She walked up to the stand, and the middle-aged man looked at her to greet her and his jaw dropped. It was Pineapple Peter himself.

"Boy, I'm sorry that I'm staring at you like this. But you look exactly like an old friend of mine that I went to school with in Hana. Sorry, it must just be a coincidence," said Pineapple Peter. "Ice cream's on me. What flavor can I get you? Lilikoi is really good."

"Oh, that's not necessary." Lani had to catch herself as well. Was this really a coincidence, or did she look like someone, her mother, great-aunt or someone else and he knew them?

"I insist," he said with a smile on his face. "Just for old time's sake. She was a close friend of mine back in school, and one day she suddenly disappeared…"
Lani didn't really want to talk to him about her mother or great-aunt and the house right now, so she just changed the subject. "I really could use some coffee if you have some. I just got here yesterday and have wicked jet lag."

"Sure. I don't sell it, but I have some of my own. I hope you like your coffee with milk?"
She nodded. He turned around and unscrewed the top of a thermos and poured some coffee into the top that could be used as a cup as well and hadn't been used yet.

"And I'll have the lilikoi ice cream, please. But please let me pay for it," she added.
She took a big sip of coffee. "This coffee is really good!"

"It's 100% Hawaiian coffee, grown Upcountry near Makawao. If you have time, you should really go and visit. It's beautiful up there." He stared at her and asked again. "You don't happen to know a woman named Luana Kalekilio, do you? You seriously look exactly like her…"
She had no idea who he was talking about. She wondered if there was a connection, but didn't want to talk about it right now.

He added: "If you ever hear from her, please let me know. I'd love to know what happened to her. As I said, she was a very good friend." He grabbed a receipt pad and wrote his phone number on it and handed the piece of paper to Lani. "Just in case, you never know."

Lani wasn't ready for this yet. But Maui was a small island and she realized that people probably knew her mother and father and she might soon find out what had happened to them and why she was given up for adoption. She needed to leave. She got a five dollar bill out of her wallet and put it on the counter.

"Please, it's my treat," said Peter, but when she insisted, he said "OK, I'll accept it for the fund supporting all the stray cats around here" and pointed smiling at a few cats about fifty feet away from the stand, sitting under a tree in the shade. "You take care and mahalo. It was nice to meet you."

"Luana...", Lani mumbled in her thoughts, as she pulled back out onto the Hana Highway. "Who knows, maybe that's my mother...different last name though." She made sure to put the note with Peter's phone number in a safe place. She might need it again to ask him some questions...

Chapter 10

Lani finally passed the HANA town sign and came up to a stand on the right with a sign that said *Maui Farms*. This was the stand that Pike Kahananui had recommended her to stop at for fruits and vegetables. Some nice young people from all over the world greeted her. They were all here working with the workaway program, meaning they were working on the farm in Hana and staying there for free, with free meals and pocket money.

"What an awesome opportunity to travel around the world!" said Lani as the teenagers explained the concept to her.
She picked up ripe papayas, mangoes, lilikoi (which she had never seen before), bananas, avocados and smelled them. They were so aromatic that she closed her eyes and just relished the scent. She wanted to buy all of them, but chose just a few for now. She also bought some peppers, carrots and cucumbers and then finally some coffee from Maui and some coconut candy.

"I'll be back!" she said to the group of teenagers, jumped in her little car and rushed off to her next stop, just a few hundred yards down the road from the Maui Farm stand, on the same side, Island General Store.

Lani was amazed. This store had just about everything you could imagine: t-shirts, butter, bread, fishing gear, ice cream, fruits and vegetables, meat, birthday cards… your typical small town general store that has everything. Lani picked up a few items for dinner and breakfast, and as she checked out, she looked at the older Hawaiian man at the cash register. They both had a weird feeling as their eyes met. By the look on his face, it was like a dagger had gone straight through his heart. She had a strange feeling about him too, as if she knew him. There was something tragic about him, and she strangely felt a connection to him.

"That'll be thirty two dollars and fifty two cents," Kumu Kalekilio said, as he looked up at her, awestruck, from his chair behind the register.

"Thank you very much. I'd also like to introduce myself. I'm Lani Winters. I'm staying at Koki Beach House. I'll be here for a couple of weeks, so I'll be seeing you around." He nodded silently. His eyes never left her as Lani left the store. She felt as if she had met this man before, but that didn't seem possible. Lani had heard too many different names since her arrival yesterday that she didn't make a connection between his name, the store and Pineapple Peter asking her about Luana Kalekilio.

She didn't realize that she was opening old wounds in the Kalekilio family and the entire town of Hana by coming.

Kumu quietly tried to gather himself. Koki Beach House had belonged to his estranged sister who hadn't spoken with him for 30 years. Who was this young woman? He thought he possibly knew who she was, but didn't say a thing to her. She seemed clueless. As soon as Lani had left, Kumu told his assistant Martha to take care of the store and went back to the attached house, where his wife Leila was making dinner in the kitchen. She looked up.

"You look like you just saw a ghost, Kumu. What happened?"

"I think I just saw Luana's daughter."

Kumu had to sit down. His wife's whole face dropped as well and she had to sit down, too. She had tears in her eyes as she stared at him.

"Luana's daughter?? How do you even know she had a daughter?"

"Well, there was a girl out in the store just now, in about the same age that Luana's daughter could be now. She looked exactly like Luana, except that her skin was a bit lighter, and she told me she's staying at Koki Beach House."

Leila stared at him. "I have to go and see her," she whispered.

"No, you're not going to go and see her" Kumu answered. "Let's wait and see what happens first. It might not be who I think it is."

It was Kumu's fault that their pregnant daughter had left almost 30 years ago in the middle of the night and never came back. And he never forgave himself for that. Nobody knew whether she was still alive or if she had given birth to her child. He had accused his sister Malani of helping Luana and possibly sending her to the mainland, but he had never found out where Luana went and whether she was still alive. There had also been rumors that Luana had thrown herself off of the cliffs of Lanai, but nobody could ever prove it. Now Malani was dead and with her any hope to ever get any information about Luana and her child …

Hana had never been the same, since the Luana incident happened. Just like with a bad political situation and a country splitting into two parties, the residents of Hana had been split into two sides since almost thirty years: Kumu's side that hated "Haoles", the white intruders, and never forgave Luana for becoming pregnant from one, and Malani's side that was more tolerant and thought family was more important than racism and intolerance and that Luana's ohana, her family, should have helped her instead of abandoning her and making her leave and "ruin" her life.

Lani had no idea yet what a stir she was about to cause. She drove through "downtown" Hana where she saw some other little stores, passed Henderson Ranch on the right, saw beautiful grassy meadows on both sides with cows grazing everywhere. On the left was the ocean. She took a left, stopped at Koki Beach, a red sand beach with red lava boulders on the side and the ocean roaring up to the shore, with a beautiful view onto Alau Island, an Island close to the shore that pointed out of the ocean like a giant shark's fin. There was a food truck with the famous Huli Huli chicken, which she would learn to love and end up getting quite often since she was not a very good cook. She actually decided to stop here and get some dinner even though she had just bought groceries, but she realized she'd be much too tired to cook and that Huli Huli chicken sounded really good right now.

"Can I please have one Huli Huli chicken to go," asked Lani the nice young Hawaiian girl who was working in the food truck.

"Sure. I'll pack it up for you." answered the girl. "Unfortunately, we're out of dessert already. You'll have to come back another day and try our homemade lilikoi bars. They are to die for."

"Oh, definitely! I just had lilikoi ice cream for the first time today too and it's already my favorite!"

They smiled at each other and Lani handed a twenty dollar bill to the girl. She gave her the change and said "Mahalo. See you next time." Lani replied: "Mahalo. I'm staying at Koki Beach House, which must be right up the road. I'll be seeing you around. I'm Lani. Nice to meet you."

"I'm Malea. Nice to meet you," replied the girl in the food truck. "Koki Beach House? That's Malani's house…"

"I'm her great niece. It looks like I inherited the house, but I have to renovate it within a certain time or it's going to be sold to some investor."

"Wow, what a shame that would be. Malani would certainly not want that and I'm sure the people of Hana would hate that. Everyone loved Malani. She was like an aunt to everyone. She never had her own kids, but she always had these gigantic parties for everyone in town. Too bad she passed away. We all miss her."
Lani nodded.

"Well, I'll see you next time. I hope you can renovate the house. It's awesome," said Malea.

"Thanks. See you next time."

… Another half mile through a residential area and she took a left into the driveway of Koki Beach House, with gigantic plumerias on both sides.

She was immediately enchanted by the beautiful tropical gardens and the view out on to the ocean that she had from almost everywhere in the yard. She had been told to look for the caretaker Max in the guesthouse. She knocked, but nobody was there. She walked up to the front door, tried the door handle and, since it was unlocked, she stepped inside…

The entire house was made of very dark wood and at first it made quite a dark impression, but as soon as she stepped into the main living area, a live-in kitchen opening up to a big living room with two story vaulted ceilings and an entire sunny glass front facing out onto the ocean, she was enchanted by the beauty of the older house. She stepped out onto the back porch and could feel the salt of the ocean in the air. She just stood there, breathing, listening to the roaring of the mighty Pacific. What a beautiful place this was. It certainly wasn't the small shack in the jungle she had seen in her nightmares. She had to laugh about those nightmares she had been having. After a while, she turned around and stepped back into the house. She noticed the centerpiece of the house on the living-room wall: A big oil painting of a young woman sitting in the sand on a beach, surrounded by dark boulders, coconut fronds and other tropical plants. She froze. The woman in the painting looked exactly like **HER**.

Chapter 11
Flashback, Hana 1988, thirty years ago

Just like Georgia O'Keeffe in 1939, painters from the mainland had always been drawn to Maui to paint the tropical foliage, colorful flowers and beautiful landscapes, trying to capture the unique magic of Maui in their paintings. One of these artists, a tall, handsome, yet very quiet man from Upstate New York named Paul Kent, had rented a little cabin a few hundred yards from Waioka Pond for the summer and spent every moment either driving around, looking for new projects to paint, or working on a new piece of art – or hanging out at his favorite place, Hamoa Beach.

One day, when he had stopped to buy some groceries at the Island General Store in Hana, he saw Luana Kalekilio, the owner's daughter, working there, restocking the shelves. Paul was immediately mesmerized by her classic beauty, and even though he was usually shy, he couldn't help himself, and had to walk over to talk to her, to try to start a conversation.

"Aloha," he said with a deep, pleasant tenor voice.
She looked up and smiled at the handsome stranger.

"Aloha." She immediately turned around and checked where her father was, because she knew that he tolerated Haoles in his store, because he needed them for his business, but probably not when they spoke with his daughter...
Paul cut straight to the chase.

"I'm an artist and I'm working on a painting of Hamoa Beach with all of the tropical plants down there... I still need a model. You'd totally fit in. Would you be interested in sitting to model for me?"

In this instance, Luana's father stepped back into the store. Luana was flattered and didn't see that her father had returned. She thought this guy with the blue eyes and the fair hair was quite handsome. She smiled, but didn't have a chance to answer, because Kumu had already stormed up and grabbed her not very gently by her arm and pulled her into the house that was in back of the store.

"I don't want you flirting with that Haole, okay?" he said with a harsh voice.

"I wasn't flirting. He just asked me a question and I answered it." Luana defended herself.

"Don't talk to him ever again." said Kumu sharply.
Leila, Luana's mother, walked up and asked: "What's going on here?"

"Our daughter is flirting with Haoles like some floozy!" Kumu answered sharply. "Don't ever talk to that man again." he hissed at Luana and returned to the store.
Luana burst out in tears and her mother took her in her arms.

"I wasn't flirting, mom, he just asked me a question and I answered. I'm not a floozy."

"Okay, my darling. I believe you. And don't listen to that language. It's unacceptable. Just make sure Dad doesn't catch you talking to him again. Shhh, shhhh, it's okay… I hope Dad didn't just lose a customer. We need every one we can get". A third general store had been just opened in "downtown" Hana and Kalekilios had already noticed a decline in customers. She tried to calm her daughter down. The older Luana got, the less she could stand her father's behavior. He was so intolerant and bull-headed, she didn't even understand how her mother could be married to him. Thank goodness, she always had her Aunt Malani to talk to and confide in when she had problems. Her Aunt Malani was her father's much younger sister who was more like a big sister than an Aunt to her and sometimes it felt like she spent more time with her than with her own parents…

Paul Kent had already left the store, shocked about Mr. Kalekilio's unfriendly behavior following an innocent conversation and was driving over to one of the other stores, just as Leila had suspected. He certainly wasn't going to go shopping at the Island General Store anymore, even if the girl that worked there was gorgeous.

Chapter 12

After Luana and her parents had calmed down, she didn't think much of this encounter anymore and forgot about Paul Kent, until, a few days later, it was her day off and she went to Hamoa Beach with a few girlfriends. It was a beautiful day in paradise.

Luana and her friends Alana, Kai and Leilani jumped out of the old pick up truck that Luana had borrowed from her parents with the Island General Store sign on the side, grabbed their towels and beach bags off of the trucks' cargo area and walked down the steps to Hamoa Beach, which lay before them like a perfect crescent, surrounded by lush tropical vegetation and cliffs on both sides. They carelessly dropped their towels and bags into the sand, pulled their shorts and sundresses off, threw them down on a pile and ran down to the sparkling water.

"Last gets bitten by the dogs!" yelled Luana and ran into the wild refreshing waves.

"Wait for me!" yelled Alana, while she and the other girls followed, splashing each other and frolicking about happily like four little puppies. They body surfed until they were tired and then they walked back up to the beach, spread their towels out and sunbathed, chatting happily, looking over at a group of boys on the side of the beach, secretly smoking a first cigarette. It was summer vacation, they all had a summer job, either at Hana Hotel, Henderson Ranch or, like Luana, at her parents' store, and they had all planned their days off on the same days to get to spend some time together.

Luana noticed the tall handsome young artist from the store standing under the shady trees in the back of the beach behind his easel, facing the other way, concentrating on his painting. He hadn't noticed them yet. The ocean was so loud that most noises were drowned out. She was curious, quickly pulled her sundress over and walked over to look at his painting.

"Hey there!" she said.

He looked up, a bit startled, but then he recognized her and smiled.

"Oh, sorry, I was concentrating and didn't hear you come up. How are you?"

"I'm good. I'm sorry about my dad's behavior in the store."

"That's okay. Maybe I'd behave the same way if my beautiful daughter was talking to some Haole who just walked up and said he wanted to paint her," he replied with a grin.

"Well, he was quite rude. And I apologize. I'm Luana, by the way."

"I'm Paul."

She looked at the painting. It was quite stunning, in an impressionistic technique, very colorful and cheery. It made her smile.

"I love your painting."

"Thank you. I'd love to paint you one day," he replied.

He had to stare at her beautiful features again, which made her blush a little.

"You'd look stunning in this painting. Would you mind if I took a photo of you?"

"Sure, why not?"

He fished an old manual camera out of his backpack, put it in focus and took a few photos of her, while he gave her some instructions on how to pose.

"I'd love to show you the photos if you're around in a few days. And maybe I can make a few sketches and show them to you too."

"Sure. I'd love to see them. My next day off is Tuesday. We'll be back here. I have to get back to my friends now."

"Nice to meet you."

"Bye. Gotta go," she replied breathlessly, turned around and hurried back to her friends who were already packing up their things, ready to leave. The girls teased Luana. "It looks like you have an admirer!" They laughed. Luana blushed again.

"Don't tell my dad. He'll kill me if he finds out that I talked to that guy again!" Luana urged them. "He was really nice…" she said quietly, as they walked back up the stairs, got back into the pick up and drove off, back toward Hana. They all smiled, giggled and looked back down at the beach to see if they could catch one more glimpse of Luana's new crush.

Chapter 13

Luana returned to Hamoa Beach quite a lot on her next days off and before or after work. She couldn't stop thinking of the handsome painter, and he couldn't stop thinking of her either. He developed the photos in the cabin's bathroom that he had set up as a dark room. They were stunning. Luana was a classic beauty and Paul was not only a great painter, he was also a gifted photographer. He drew some sketches of her, started some portraits and also added her to the painting he had been working on down on Hamoa Beach. It became his masterpiece.

After a while, Luana's friends didn't accompany her anymore. She started coming by herself. She wanted to have more time with Paul and to be alone with him. They could talk and talk for hours and could also just be still when he was concentrating on his painting. One day, they just sat silently on Hamoa Beach, watching the sun set behind the hills, while the sky was illuminated in all shades of pink, orange and red. They couldn't stop looking into each other's eyes and were drawn to each other. Finally, they both leaned in for a tender kiss that became more and more passionate. Luana was a bit shocked that she had let her feelings go this far. She put her hand in front of her mouth, jumped up and whispered:

"If my dad finds out…!"

Before Paul could answer, she gathered up her bag, flip-flops and hoodie and rushed up the path to the street. She tried to stay away from him for a few days but she couldn't help herself. She missed him, the conversations with him, his smile, the way he looked at her, the way he touched her, and especially the kiss.

A few days later, she suddenly showed up at his studio near Waioka Pond. He was surprised, because they had never talked about where he was staying and they had certainly never been there. But Hana was a small town. She had asked some of the locals and they knew where he was staying. She walked around the studio, looking at all the sketches and paintings of her that he was working on. He took her hand, led her through the little studio and made signs for her to sit down on a chair by the window that the sun was shining into. He got behind his easel that was also right there and started drawing a sketch of her. It was all very intimate and romantic. She sat there, watched him work and loved every minute of it. They never said a single word. When he was done with his sketch, he walked up to her chair, pulled her up and started kissing her. They slowly moved toward the bed where they made love, at first very gently, but then more and more passionately.

They both fell asleep and took a wonderful peaceful nap, their arms and legs intertwined in each other. Paul woke up and just lay there, looking at her beautiful classic Polynesian face. Finally, she opened her eyes and smiled.

"Hey, sleepy head," he said gently, "are you hungry?"
She nodded, while she yawned and stretched.
He walked over to the fridge and got out some Italian bread, salami, mozzarella, tomatoes, peppers and olives and put everything on a tray, which he brought over to the bed. He made one big sandwich for both of them. They both took turns taking bites of it with a big appetite.

"I've never eaten food like this. It's delicious," said Luana.

"These are all Italian specialties. I'd love to take you to Italy one day." he replied and smiled at her. She smiled back at him and nodded. She liked that idea.

"Let's walk over to Waioka Pond and go for a swim," he proposed when they were done eating.
Luana shook her head. After they had made love for the first time, she was even more nervous than usual about someone seeing them together and telling her father.

"What if someone sees us and tells my father," she answered. "Let's go swimming in the Pools of 'Ohe'o or even further, where less people know me."

Paul looked at his watch. It was noon. They had the entire afternoon before sundown, so they could still go for a ride.

They started driving toward the West side of Maui, where nobody knew Luana and she could show him new beautiful painting spots.

Luana did her work just like she was supposed to and never got in trouble so that her father wouldn't ask questions or become suspicious. She told her parents she was going out with her friends or hanging out at Aunt Malani's, and Malani, who she told about Paul, and Luana's best friend Alana covered for her. She and Paul only had two full days a week with each other and either mornings or evenings, depending on whether Luana had to work early or late, but they loved every minute and made the best of it. They just lived in the moment and went wherever they felt like going.

Chapter 14

One day they drove all the way to the west coast of Maui, via Piilani Highway, all the way out of the rain forest, through the rugged outskirts of the dormant volcano Haleakala, where millions of years ago lava had flown into the ocean after Haleakala had erupted. Remaining were harsh hills, valleys and canyon ridges that looked like they were on a different planet. Paul drove and Luana rode shotgun and gave him directions. She had Paul stop at the Kaupo Store to show him their collection of antique cameras and to get some drinks and snacks. As they continued their drive through this remote area, they had to slow down on the rattling slats of the cattle guards. They watched herds of cattle passing or walking ahead of them and laughed boisterously when Luana imitated the mooing cows. They stopped at Huakini Bay and walked down to the beautiful black rock beach and they just sat there and listened to the zen-like sounds of the waves going over the rocks. They stopped for beautiful coastal views of Molokini and Lanai in the ocean stretching out on the left side.

Finally, they left the rugged area and arrived in Upcountry and at the 'Unalupa Ranch Store'. Even though they both didn't have a lot of money and mostly brought a picnic, they had to stop here for one of the grass-fed hamburgers that were grilled right outside the store and famous on the entire island. They left Kula, the cowboy town Makawoa and Paia aside, because it was still quite far to their destination, Honolua Bay, which they could only reach by walking down a beautiful enchanted path with giant banyan trees on both sides. Luana looked up into one of the trees and it looked like a thousand shimmering ropes were hanging down from the tree. These were air roots with the rays of the sun shining on them. They had to take their shoes off and wade through a stream, which of course led to Luana splashing Paul and him splashing back and then they paused, looked into each other's eyes for what seemed like an eternity and then finally kissed each other again… they got back onto the path and were greeted by a group of chickens, with a rooster in tow, which ran ahead of them, clucking loudly. Then the chickens disappeared back in the long grass in between the trees. Paul had his camera around his neck and took what felt like hundreds of pictures. They got their snorkeling gear out of their backpacks, jumped into the refreshing water of Honolua Bay and slowly glided along beautiful colorful fishes. Luana showed him where to swim until they reached the reef and saw coral and more fishes. Suddenly, she got very excited and her eyes widened, when she spotted a Humuhumunukunukaupua'a, the state fish of Hawaii, and pointed it out to him under water.

They had to leave Honolua Bay soon, because the drive back to Hana would take at least three to four hours and they still had to go to one spot that Luana wanted to show Paul: Nakalele Blowhole and Maui's heart shaped rock, Sweetheart Rock. They stopped on the side of the road and followed a hiking trail leading down to the ocean, where they first came to a blowhole. Paul was already on his way all the way down the blowhole, when Luana called him back, telling him it was too dangerous and slippery and that big waves washed over the entire area sometimes.

He stopped and they looked to the right where they saw the perfect heart hole in a boulder, about three feet above the ground, with the ocean in the background. Sweetheart Rock. Paul kissed Luana. And again, he had to grab his camera and take countless photos of her.

The drive back to Hana was tough this time, they didn't arrive until after dark and the road to Hana was dangerous, but Paul found it almost easier to drive in the dark because he could see the headlights of the oncoming cars and be aware of them. This time, Luana snuck into the house, while her parents were watching TV in the living-room, and when her mother came upstairs to check on her, she pretended to be asleep...

Chapter 15

Paul and Luana never got tired of spending time together, but the day of Paul's departure moved closer and closer.

"My flight back to New York is next week. I had to take this job as a tour guide in the Thousand Islands. I've been spending money all summer and I'm quite broke now and have to replenish my bank account before the fall. The season in New York will be over soon. Can you imagine it starts getting cold in September?"
She looked at him with her big brown eyes and sighed. She couldn't imagine the place he was from that seemed so beautiful in summer, but then for nine months it was rainy, bitter cold and covered in snow.

"I don't know what I'll do when you're gone… Stay here! Or take me with you!" she blurted out.
She became quite obsessed with the idea of going with him, because then she'd be away from her father, but she knew how unrealistic it was. Paul was more pragmatic.

"I'll come back next summer. We'll stay in touch and time will fly."
Her face became gloomy. She didn't think so, but there was nothing she could do.

On the day of Paul's departure, they were both heartbroken. She helped him pack up the small cabin. He had already shipped most of his paintings home and some were actually exhibited in the lobby of the Hana Hotel. Luana was in a gloomy mood, and Paul did his best to cheer her up.

"Come here. I have a surprise for you!"
She walked over with a hanging head.

"This is for you." He handed Luana a smaller beautiful portrait of herself, surrounded by tropical foliage. "I know you will have to hide it for now. But maybe one day you can hang it up in our home that we'll have together. For now, you can look at it from time to time and think of us."

He also handed her a big manila envelope with her name on it. Inside was a collection of beautiful photos of her, him and the two of them together that people had taken of them on their many excursions. She started crying.

"These are beautiful. And I have nothing for you," she sobbed.

"Your love is all I need," he replied and gave her a kiss.

They just stood there in the empty cabin, hugging each other.

"It's time to go," Paul said and lifted his heavy suitcase, carry-on and camera case onto the back of his pick-up truck. They departed in the pick-up truck and stopped briefly at Hamoa Beach, because Paul and Luana wanted to say a quick goodbye to their favorite place. They just sat in the car on the side of the road and looked down at the ocean, through the palm tree fronds.

"The hours we spent here were beautiful." Paul said. "I'm going to miss this place."

"I won't be able to ever come here by myself." Luana said. "It will be so sad without you."

"Please enjoy it. Come back with your friends. I'll be waiting for your updates on what's going on here and I want to know that you're happy."

Finally, they also had to leave Hamoa Beach and slowly drove through Hana. Luana always ducked a little when they passed the Island General Store and she did it again this time. At the exit of town, a bit past the Maui Farms' stand, Paul stopped and had to let Luana out. Island General Store was so close that she could walk home. Paul turned the engine off, got out with Luana and gave her a long hug. She was crying, his eyes were teary as well. He reached around his neck and took his beautiful Hawaiian Makau fish hook necklace off and put it around Luana's neck.

"This will be your good luck charm. I'll call you tomorrow afternoon when I'm home. And I'll see you next year."

"I love you," she said through her tears.

"I love you too," he replied, got in the pick-up and drove away.

She didn't even know how long she just stood there, staring at the curve where the pick-up truck had disappeared. Slowly, she walked over to the Maui Farms stand where her friend Alana, who knew what was going on, just took her in her arms and held her.
She knew how heartbroken her friend was…

Chapter 16

Luana was not the same after Paul left. She asked her parents for additional shifts and in her spare time she just sat in her room or at Aunt Malani's house moping. Or she actually did go to Hamoa Beach, but she went by herself and just sat there, day dreaming of the past few weeks which now felt like a dream. The only time she was happy was when she could talk to Paul on the phone. This was quite difficult, though. Nobody had mobile phones in 1988 and Paul couldn't call Luana on the house phone, so the only time they could speak was when she called him from a public phone. The time difference between Hawaii and Upstate New York and both of their jobs didn't make things easier…

School started again. This was Luana's senior year and her grades were really important for her graduation. She studied as much as she could, but soon she started becoming sick every morning. Her mother and she thought she had picked up a virus that had been going around, but it wouldn't stop. She seemed to have a stomach issue and was missing too much school. Finally, her mother took her to the doctor, who quickly diagnosed that she was pregnant. It was too obvious. Luana's mother and Luana briefly thought about not telling Kumu, but there was no sense of doing that because he'd find out sooner or later. He was absolutely enraged and rampaged through the house.

"A baby from a Haole! Another Hawaiian girl lost to one of the white men who think they can have everything they want when they come here, including our women," he clamored. "Ohana and keiki mean everything to Hawaiians, but we will not have a child from a Haole in this house".

Luana yelled back at him: "I'm 18. I do what I want!" and stormed up to her room.

He yelled after her: "No, you don't! Not as long as you live under my roof!"

Even though this went against the Polynesian rules of supporting family, Kumu started trying to talk Luana into having an abortion. Hawaiian abortion laws were less restrictive than those in many other states, so he thought it would be pretty easy. When Luana refused to speak with her doctor about it, Kumu spoke with the healer, Ana Kamealoha, who lived on the Road Past Hana, out by Charles Lindbergh's grave, and asked her for herbs that would abort the baby. It was early in the pregnancy and he was determined that Luana was not going to ruin her future. Ana refused to give him herbs, because in her opinion it was Luana's own decision and not her father's. But Kumu felt strongly that his family's reputation would be ruined. People would find out. He was beside himself. Even though Luana was scared to death to have a baby as young as she was, she couldn't imagine getting rid of Paul's child and she refused to obey her father. She locked herself in her room for days, crying. She didn't know what to do. Her mother, father and Aunt Malani argued. Malani was against an abortion and said that Luana should be supported in having the child and it was her own choice what to do.

"Even if this child is from a Haole, it's one of our own! It's your grandchild!" Malani shouted. "How can you make her have an abortion?! You have to help your daughter! And if you don't want to help her yourself, then she can move in with me!"

"There will be no half-breed in our family!" he shouted. "And look at this!"
He slapped a New York Times onto the kitchen table with a photo of Paul Kent with a beautiful woman at his side, at a gallery opening in New York City. "He just used her as his island fling."

Luana's mother and Malani just stared at the newspaper and couldn't reply.
Kumu continued: "He's probably married and will never come back." He threw the newspaper into the recycling bin and Malani left without saying a word.

Luana, who was upstairs in her room listening, perked her ears. What was he talking about? Later, when her parents were asleep, she snuck down, looked for the newspaper, found it in the recycling bin next to the stove in the kitchen and looked at the article her father had mentioned. It was clearly Paul and he clearly had his arm around this beautiful woman's shoulders. Luana put the newspaper back, quietly and slowly, with tears running down her cheeks. She walked back upstairs like in a trance and threw herself on her bed, crying. She was determined to run away and have the baby somewhere else anyway, but she never called Paul Kent again.

Luana's best friend Alana, who supported Luana in everything she did, Aunt Malani and Luana had a secret meeting. Malani told them about her plan for Luana to hide in Lanai until she had the baby or until it was too late for an abortion.

"So, I talked to my friends in Lanai. They need someone to help out as a nanny. They have three little kids and run a bed & breakfast. Their nanny just left and the mom can't handle all the work by herself. Do you think you are well enough to do that? It might be pretty tough for someone who's pregnant. Taking care of three kids is not easy."
Luana nodded.

"I think I can handle that. I'm used to lifting heavy things in the store and working a lot."

Anything sounded better than staying with her parents right now. Malani continued. "I'd say Alana drives you to Lahaina, while I stay in Hana, just in case your dad discovers that you're gone before the ferry leaves. I'd be able to distract him and you and the baby will be in safety."

"Thanks, Aunt Malani!" Luana felt a bit positive for the first time she had found out that she was pregnant. At least she had a plan now. She gave her aunt a hug.

"You can stay there until you have the baby. Then we can go from there," said Malani.

Chapter 17

A few days later, before sunrise, a dark shadow snuck out of the back of the Island General Store, carrying just a duffel bag and a purse. Luana walked over to the Maui Farms stand where Alana was waiting for her in Malani's car to take her to Lahaina where the ferry to Lanai departed once a day in the morning. Luana and Malani hugged each other and said a tearful goodbye. From Lahaina, Luana took the very first ferry to Lanai. Lanai was a sleepy little island before a couple of big resorts opened in 2005 and made the island busier. Luana stepped off the ferry and was picked up by a man and woman in a truck. Luana was now not only having a baby from a Haole, but living with Haoles too.

Paul couldn't reach Luana anymore. He tried calling the store several times, but hung up when Luana's parents answered the phone. He had no other way of getting in touch with her and she had decided to not tell him about the baby, since she was convinced that he was married or in a relationship and had only used her as a vacation fling.

Even though Elizabeth and Brandon Smith, her hosts, were very sweet people, working as a nanny for three children was quite tough for Luana in her condition. Two of the children were still in diapers and the other one was very energetic, and it was non-stop work all day, until Elizabeth was done working at the hotel reception desk and could take over. On many evenings, Luana just fell asleep on her bed, exhausted from all of the running around she had to do all day. It got tougher and tougher for her, the bigger her unborn baby became…

It didn't help that she was quite homesick and didn't know what was going to happen with her and the baby. She had basically made up her mind to give the baby up for adoption, but didn't even think she wanted to return to Hana after her family had treated her the way they did, because she had supposedly ruined their reputation… She had always dreamed of going to college in Honolulu and becoming a landscape architect or having a nursery. Maybe she could take the baby to the adoption agency there, find a job and go back to school one day.

Four weeks before her due date, she suddenly became dizzy while making the children's beds and she passed out, falling to the floor in a heap. It took a while until the oldest child found her, tried to wake her up and then ran down to his mother to inform her about what had happened to Luana.

Luana was rushed to Lanai's Community Hospital. Due to the fall, her water had broken and the baby, a healthy, but tiny little girl weighing in at almost five pounds, had to be induced and delivered early. Mama Luana and baby, so far no name, were well and resting in the hospital. No one except Elizabeth and Brandon visited her. They tried to reach Malani, but she was out of town and nobody answered the phone at her house.

Luana wasn't well at all. She was extremely depressed. She couldn't look at the baby, stared into thin air all day, tears running down her cheeks, all she could think of, was her and Paul at Hamoa Beach and all of the beautiful memories they had and then the newspaper article with Paul and the other woman. Elizabeth and Brandon tried to talk to her and give her hope in her desperate situation. They were finally able to reach Malani who rushed to Lanai as quickly as she could, but it wasn't a quick trip from Hana.

"Malani is on her way." Elizabeth told Luana. "She will be here tomorrow morning and she is going to help you. Don't give up hope now. You have come this far. Look at your beautiful baby daughter. She needs you."

"I don't want to see anybody," replied Luana, hopeless, her eyes red from the tears that flowed endlessly

The next morning, before the night shift changed to day shift and before Malani could make it to Lanai, Luana put on her clothes and quietly snuck out of the hospital. She didn't even look at the baby. She walked out of town and hitchhiked to the area of the cliffs by Puu Pehe and was last seen by a hiker standing at the cliffs. It seemed like she might have jumped off of the cliffs, but we never found out whether she did or not. That was the last anyone ever saw of Luana.

Malani arrived too late at the hospital. All she found was the baby that the nurses were taking care of until someone from Child Protective Services came or until family claimed her. Malani took the baby, respected Luana's wish and brought her to an adoption agency in Honolulu the same day, so that her brother and his wife wouldn't interfere. In Luana's room at the Lanai Bed & Breakfast, Malani and the Smiths found the manila envelope with the photos Paul had given Luana. Malani decided to keep them in a safe place for the baby in case she ever made it back to Maui one day...

Chapter 18
Back to Present Time – Hana

Max, 30, the house's caretaker, was a tall, sensitive, good looking young man who had been raised by his grandmother, Malani's best friend. When his grandmother died and he had just finished his training as a fire fighter after high school, he didn't really have anywhere to go and Malani offered him to live in her guesthouse.

They ended up being very good for each other: Malani had someone to watch the house and take care of the yard during her extensive travels and, since Max was very handy, she also had someone to fix things in this old house that basically always needed something repaired, and Max had someone, who of course couldn't replace his mother, but it was good to not be all alone in the world and have someone look after him…

The front door of the main house was standing wide open when Max came home. He stepped into the foyer and shouted:

"Hello! Is anybody here?"

Lani was concentrating so much on the painting she had just discovered, that she didn't even hear Max walk in. She was just standing in the middle of the great room, staring at the painting of the beautiful woman who looked exactly like her. The sun was shining on her hair, and Max was shocked to see this beautiful woman who appeared to have just stepped out of the painting and was looking back at herself. Max had a hard time getting words out.

Lani took a closer look at the painting and tried to decipher the initials on the bottom right – it looks like "*PK*" and then the year "*88*" (her year of birth…) …

"Hi, Lani?" Max tried to get her attention.

She looked at him, like in a daze, but shook off her emotions, walked up to him and stretched out her hand to shake his. There certainly was a moment of tension when their eyes met for the first time.

"Hi, you must be Max. I'm Lani. Do you know who that is in that painting and where it's from? Isn't that crazy? It looks exactly like me!"

"Yes, it does. To be honest with you, I always thought it was Malani as a young girl. It's always been there." A mystery, but of course it could really be Malani and Lani could look like a mirror image of her great-aunt, but something didn't make sense …

"The thing is, this says the painting was painted in 1988 and from what I understand, my Great Aunt Malani was much older than this in 1988… but, of course the painter could have also used an old photo," said Lani. She was pretty sure that the girl in the painting was her mother and was already obsessed with finding out more about her and what could have happened to her – and if she was dead or alive.

Max was more practical and not as interested in who the person in the painting was.

"You must be tired from your long trip from Kahului. I picked up some take-out for dinner. Are you hungry?"

"Funny that you should mention that. I got a few groceries at the store, but picked up some take-out too, because it looked so good and I thought it might be too much work to cook tonight."
It turned out that they had both gotten Huli Huli chicken from the only place between here and Hana town, but also a very good choice.
They sat at a wooden picnic table out on the porch, overlooking the ocean and unwrapped two of the three portions.

"This is the best chicken around." Max said with a charming smile. "I hope you like it." He had a soft voice, typical for Hawaiians, with a slight accent.

They ate silently for a while. The food was delicious. But Lani was tired. Max tried to break the silence.

"How was your drive from Hana?"

"Ohhhh… it was so beautiful," she started gushing about the views and tropical foliage and everything she had seen. "I'm in love. It's a dangerous road, sure, but it's not so bad if you take your time and drive carefully."

"Yes, it's beautiful. I agree. It's not that bad – there are some areas on the back road leading to Upcountry that are much more dangerous."

"Oh, that's if you continue past Hana and don't go back to Paia?"

"Yes. I'm off tomorrow. I work as a fire fighter for the Hana Fire Department. I do two days of twelve-hour shifts and then have three days off. I often work on the weekends. But it's not bad. Sometimes it's nice to be off during the week when other people are working. I thought I'd take you into town tomorrow and introduce you to some people who are knowledgeable about construction and pretty good handymen. And after that, we can go for a drive on the Piilani Highway if you'd like." She smiled. She was impressed that he already had a plan.

"Sure, I'd love that. Thanks. And if there is anything you can do to help me find out about what happened to my mother, I'd greatly appreciate it."

He nodded.

"Would you like to take a look at the rest of the house, before I let you get some rest?"

She nodded. "That would be great."

"I'm a bit nervous. Is the house in very bad shape?" she asked.

"It depends on what you think is bad. There was quite some water damage a few months ago when we had some flooding, and your great-aunt wasn't financially and healthwise able to take care of it. I think that's going to be quite expensive. And some stuff here and there has to be fixed. It's definitely worth it though. The house has a good foundation and is probably worth 1.5 million dollars, including the land."

Lani's jaw dropped. She had no idea that the house was that valuable. Max saw her astounded face.

"Malani's husband was a lawyer and not poor. They bought the house about 25 years ago when property prices were still very low. In the past 10 years, especially since Oprah bought a house in Upcountry and some other celebrities settled near here, prices have skyrocketed. They had a lot of big parties and company here, but Malani's husband died very young of cancer, and it ended up being too big to handle by herself. She was also always kind of sad that she didn't have kids and she always talked about her niece who had left and whom she missed very much. She probably meant your mom with that…"

Once again, Lani thought of the painting in the great room. She wondered too.

"Probably. I guess it must have been her too…"

"Maybe. I don't know." Max answered. "Your great-aunt Malani was a wonderful person. She and my kupunawahine were best friends and I spent a lot of time here. This was always our first stop when we went to Hamoa Beach and she had fabulous parties, especially for all of the kids in town since she didn't have her own. She even did fundraisers here for the schools and kids in need."

They walked over to the sunny open kitchen with dark wooden cabinets. He waved for Lani to look under the counter on the outside of the kitchen and at the wall where some old water stains were quite visible.

"I'm not sure how difficult it's going to be to dry this out, but I'm afraid that the entire wall might have to be replaced."
Lani was shocked. It did look pretty bad, although it was only noticeable if you knew about it. But of course there could also be mold underneath...

Besides the kitchen and the living-/dining-room, there were a little guest bathroom, a master bath and a master bedroom downstairs. The master bath also had some water damage. Not from flooding, but from broken water pipes. It was so bad, that currently the water leading to the bathroom had been shut off and only the upstairs bathroom could be used. The master bedroom was quaint and beautiful, decorated with Polynesian furniture and with windows facing out toward the ocean and into the garden.

Before they went upstairs, Max walked over to the kitchen and poured them both another glass of wine.

"This might help you cope with the damage in the house for now, although upstairs is not as bad," he laughed as he handed her a glass. She laughed thankfully while she took the glass. She liked him already.

Upstairs were two further big bedrooms with two queen-size beds each, both also furnished with old Polynesian furniture and with beautiful views and a second bathroom. Between the two bedrooms was an open landing looking down into the great room, which had been turned into a little reading area with two rattan armchairs and glass tables, and a little office facing the front of the house. There were some other smaller paintings in the same style as the big one downstairs and with the initials *PK* throughout the house. Lani was amazed about all of the paintings. They must have been quite valuable. The upper floor didn't really look like it was in bad shape, but then Max informed her that the house urgently needed a new roof. The roof in the guesthouse was already leaking, it was covered with some tarps right now, and the garage needed some work as well. Lani was quite overwhelmed. Between the money she had gotten from her parents and what she might get for selling her nursery, but then having to deduct what she owed Michael, it would probably still not be enough.

"Well, you must be exhausted, after flying in yesterday and your long drive today. I have some stuff I need to take care of tonight and I'll let you get some rest. Could you be ready to leave at 9 in the morning?" Lani was still doing the calculations in her head and didn't reply immediately.

"Lani?"

"Umm, what?"

"Is it okay if we leave at 9 am tomorrow morning?"

"Yes, of course. Thank you for doing all this!"

"No problem. I owe Malani. She was like a mom to me. And I'm quite lucky that I can live here in this piece of paradise. Good night!"

He walked down the stairs, set his glass down on the kitchen counter, opened and closed the front door and was gone. She heard his footsteps on the wooden walkway in the breezeway and another door being opened and closed. Weird to have a stranger living right there, but being all alone in this quite big house that was basically open toward the ocean side might have been a bit scary without him too. And by now, he didn't feel like a stranger. Quite the opposite ...

Lani walked through the house that was dark by now, with her glass of wine still in her hand. She turned some lights on and just looked around and listened to the roaring waves of the Pacific. She felt quite strange all by herself in this place at the end of the world.

She ended up in front of the big painting again, sat down in the big sectional, finished her glass of wine and just listened to the sound of the waves crashing against the rocks and the noisy cicadas in the yard. As soon she leaned back and her head hit the back of the couch, she was asleep.

Chapter 19

The next morning, Lani was awake very early again due to her jet lag and, to her surprise, she had fallen asleep on the couch in the living-room and had slept there all night. This time she was excited to be up so early, since she had so much to explore and see. It was 6 am, so she had three hours until she was scheduled to drive to Hana with Max. She walked through the overgrown yard down to the water, sat down on the old swing and watched the waves, while the sun came up over the sparkling water. Then she toured the entire yard and looked at all of the amazing plants that she loved and only knew as potted plants from home. Heliconia, hibiscus, bird of paradise, all sorts of ginger - variegated, awapuhi, Hawaiian red ginger as well as gigantic wooded plumerias. There were even some orchids attached to the trees. Wow, she thought wistfully … to be able to grow these outside all year round, and not have to have a heated greenhouse… There was a vine that was growing over everything which had egg-like fruit hanging from it. She picked one up from the ground and wasn't sure what it was, but it looked like the lilikoi at the stand yesterday. There was even an abandoned old vegetable garden with some old overgrown tomato plants and herbs next to the house. And pineapples. Beautiful pineapple plants full of ripe pineapples. She ran back to the house to get a knife and cut one off. In the back, by the water, were some tall coconut palms and there were coconuts all over the lawn. She went back inside and had some toast, coffee and a piece of pineapple, while she called her parents.

Lynn answered the phone with an upbeat voice.

"Lynn Winters!"

"Hey, Mom, it's me! Sorry, yesterday was so busy that I forgot to call before it was too late and you guys were already asleep. I get so confused with the time difference."

"Oh, honey, how are you? I'm so glad to hear your voice! How is everything going so far? How is the house?"

"Oh, Mom, it's paradise. Everything is so beautiful. The house is gorgeous. But it needs a lot of work. I don't even know if I can afford to fix it up. It needs a new roof, has a lot of water damage and one bathroom is totally unusable. It's quite valuable though."

"Maybe you can talk to Dad about it. He might have some good ideas. Although he won't know how much building supplies and labor in Hawaii are."

"Yeah, good idea. I'd love to talk to him anyhow. Is he home? You could put me on speaker phone."

"No, he started the kitchen makeover at Mathers' yesterday. But maybe he can call you tonight. You're six hours behind, right?"

"Yes, so when he's home at six, it'll be noon my time. I might be out and about, but I can still talk if I have reception. That seems to be the main problem here. The phone reception is really spotty everywhere. How's your knee?"

"It's great. I've been good about doing my exercises and going to physical therapy, so I'm getting better every day. I went and checked on your orchids yesterday. Everything's fine. In the shop too. By the way, Anne is doing a great job. The girls are right here. They say hi."

Lani tried talking to Lilly and Lucy through the phone.

"Lucy, Lilly! Hi, girls!"

They perked their ears for a second, but didn't understand and continued sniffing Lynn's hand for treats.

"I sure miss those girls, Mom! And I miss you guys too, of course!"

"We miss you too. But enjoy your time, the weather is miserable here. I'll let you go. Bye, honey!"

"Bye, Mom. I'm going to call Anne in the store now. Love you and say hi to Dad!"

"Love you! Bye, honey!"

After ending the call with her mom, Lani called Anne in the store, which she had on speed dial. Everything was fine there too and Anne was actually busy with a customer, which was always a good thing. She breathed a sigh of relief that everything was going so well at home.

She looked at the time on her phone. It was eight o'clock. The sun was just burning away the clouds and it looked very promising that it was going to be a beautiful day. Of course Lani didn't know yet that it rained off and on almost every day in Maui, especially in the East, around Hana… Max wasn't going to be there until 9 am. So she decided to go for a quick early morning swim at Hamoa Beach. She quickly changed into her bathing suit and a t-shirt dress on top of that, put on a pair of flip-flops and grabbed a towel. Then she walked the few hundred yards up the road where she could already see the beautiful crescent shaped beach surrounded by lush vegetation and lava cliffs on each side below her. It was a stunning view with the sun already high up in the sky, and it looked like she'd have the whole beach to herself. She walked down a flight of stairs, left her towel, dress and flip-flops on the little stone wall by the shower, walked down to the water through the soft warm sand and proceeded slowly into the water. It was colder than expected and also very rough. The waves almost knocked her over as she tried to get past the break. She dove underneath and started swimming. She had always loved water and the ocean and was a good swimmer. She tried swimming all the way across to the other side, but then she noticed that she was being pulled out further and further. There was a strong undertow and she started panicking a bit, got salt water into her mouth and nose and started choking.

Suddenly, she realized that someone was swimming up to her. It was Max. He called out to her to stay calm, as he got closer. He swam calmly next to her on the ocean side and slowly guided her out of the rip current. When they felt the strong tug of the current die down, they swam back to shore at an angle and then let the waves push them in. She fell into the sand, breathing hard.

"Boy, am I glad that you showed up! How did you know I was here?"

"I didn't! I happen to go swimming here every morning around this time. You were damn lucky. You could have been pulled out quite fast."

"I had no idea there are such strong rip currents!"

"Even if you're being pulled out, just keep swimming slowly, parallel to the beach. And then you slowly swim back to the shore, at an angle. The worst thing is when people start panicking."

"Well, thanks for saving my life," Lani replied.

"It is quite dangerous. Although it looks like you're a pretty good swimmer. But you should probably let me know if you're planning on going swimming this early. It's not good to be here all by yourself without a life guard." He grinned, since that was exactly what he did every day. "Do as I say and not as I do…"

They grinned at each other and there was a magical moment between them as their eyes stayed glued to each other a bit too long. She took in the sight of his muscular tanned body and the hazel eyes and his long, thick eyelashes.

They walked back up to the house next to each other.

"I'll see you here in thirty minutes." he said while he took a right into the guesthouse and she took a left to the main building.

Chapter 20

When Lani came back outside at nine, Max was already waiting in his old white banged up pick-up truck. She got into the truck and they drove through the residential neighborhood, past Koki Beach and then past Henderson Ranch on the left into "downtown" Hana.

"Hana is just a gas station, three general stores... Island General Store, a bit further down the road, and the two general stores in town. You'd think three's too much, but Island General Store specializes in selling food and lunches for the tourists going back to Kahului on the Road to Hana, so it kind of works out... Then there's a post office, a couple of little gift shops, Henderson Ranch Restaurant, the only restaurant in town besides the rather pricey restaurant The View at the Hana Hotel, the very upscale hotel in town with a gallery and gift shop. ... a bit further down the road are also two churches and the elementary school, oh, and then there are several food trucks and ice cream and fruit stands. A few miles down the road are the police and fire station, a small hospital and the middle and high school, also a nursery, oh and there's also a very small airport on the edge of town", explained Max. The mention of a nursery awoke Lani's curiosity. She definitely had to go and visit that.

Max continued:

"Even though we have the three small general stores, the locals get most of their groceries and supplies in Kahului. The local stores are quite expensive since everything has to be trucked in."

"How does a truck get here from Kahului? I can't imagine how any bigger vehicle can drive on the road to Hana?" she asked.

"Oh, trust me, they can. I actually used to be a truck driver for a little while before I trained to be a fire fighter. People respect you in a truck and they make sure to get the hell out of the way," he laughed. "But I've been in a few tricky situations in some really tight curves..."

She couldn't imagine and she stared at him with wide, open eyes.

Max continued. "Lots of the business people here are handymen, carpenters and contractors either fulltime or on the side, because you end up having to do a lot by yourself in such a small town. Some of the guys who work at Henderson Ranch are pretty handy. I want to introduce you to a couple of friends of mine, and they can come over and take a look at the house and give you an estimate."

She nodded. "Thank you. I appreciate that. I'd never know where to start by myself."

They drove up a little hill, parked the car and walked over to the Henderson Ranch Store.

"My friend Keanu, who works here, is a really good handyman. We can also grab some groceries while we're here. Is there anything you forgot yesterday? Don't worry about dinner. There's an awesome Thai food truck a bit past 'Ohe'o Gulch that we can get food from later."

She nodded again. "Sounds good."

They stepped inside the store. Just like the Island General Store, this place had just about everything you could imagine with shelves from the ground up to the ceiling full of countless supplies. Max and Lani walked along the shelves and found Keanu in a storage room, where he was working with the door open. Max introduced Lani to Keanu.

"Keanu, this is Lani Winters who I told you about. Do you think you can come over and take a look and see how much work is necessary?"

"Sure", Keanu replied. My next day off is the day after tomorrow. Will that work?"

"I might be at work, but I guess I don't have to be there if you just come over and take a look. Is that okay with you, Lani?"

"Of course, I totally appreciate it."

"Okay, I'll see you on Thursday then. Is 9:30 okay?" Keanu asked.

"Sure. I hope Billy will be there too. I want you both to take a look together. If not, I'll call you to discuss a different time." said Max.

"Sure." answered Keanu.

They all nodded goodbye and shook hands again while Keanu stared at Lani....

Max noticed the stare. He knew that the entire town was already gossiping about the return of Malani's great niece and Luana's daughter.

They knew it must be her, even though there never had been any evidence that Luana had really had a baby. The older locals in Hana stopped and stared when they saw Lani – she was the mirror image of her mother back then… Hana's wound about the missing daughter was opening back up… One very old lady, who was not able to tell the past from the present, even walked up to Lani and caressed her cheek, with tears in her eyes.

"Luana, you're back…"

Max pulled her along. "Don't take that too seriously," he said. "She's about 100 years old and lives in a different world."

Lani was very confused and sad, even though she should probably expect things like this after seeing how much she looked like her mother. She felt like she was opening a can of worms, but it was obviously meant to be. Why would Malani have left the house to her if she didn't want her to return and find out what happened to her mother?

After they had walked around a little and were on their way back to the truck, Max said: "Okay, then our next stop is Hana Hotel to see my friend Billy Kalawai," and smiled at Lani.

They had to park across the street from the Hana Hotel, which was an upscale all-inclusive hotel with rooms ranging from $600 - $900 per night, depending on the season. Something none of the locals or Lani could ever afford. However, the hotel and its employees were quite popular, since it gave so much back to the community. There were Hana Hotel college scholarships, grants for businesses, they had an annual cookout for the locals and they donated a lot of money to the local schools and hospital and other organizations. The building was not so impressive at first sight, it was a flat one-story building with an open lobby and front desk, but as they walked closer, Lani saw that the lobby was very charming and sunny, due to various skylights. There were big tropical flower arrangements everywhere. In the middle was a big contemporary water fountain and there were several cozy sitting areas with couches, armchairs and glass tables made of bamboo and very heavy tropical timber. The walls were decorated with beautiful tropical paintings and Lani was automatically drawn to a collection of three paintings that were all painted in the same style as the painting in Koki Beach House. She stepped closer.

"*PK. 1990.* Again. From him or her. Painted a bit later than the one in the house," said Lani.

Max nodded. He had never noticed them before.

Max walked past the front desk, greeted the receptionist and the concierge and introduced Lani to them briefly. Then they walked out of the building, all the way past a beautiful pool and through a park-like area to the back of the property to one of the beautiful ocean front bungalows. Lani could tell that Max knew his way around and Billy had instructed him where to go. Billy was fixing the A/C in one of the rooms. Max introduced Lani and Billy. Just like Keanu, Billy was quite a bit older than Max, one of his fire-fighter coworkers who had two jobs. They made an appointment for the same time Keanu was coming.

Chapter 21

They walked back to the car and drove back to Koki Beach House.

"Do you want to take a break or do you want to just drop your groceries off and go for a drive right away?"

"I'm fine. I don't need a break." She looked at him and smiled. She was too excited and curious to sit around the house and do nothing. So, she just jumped out of the pick-up and ran into the house with her two paper bags and put the few items that had to be cooled into the fridge. Max had gotten out of the truck and followed her. He shouted into the house:

"Hey, Lani, I forgot to tell you to bring your bathing suit and a towel. We might go swimming. I'm going to go and put mine on too."

"Okay." She grabbed her small backpack with a towel and sunscreen and ran into the bedroom to grab her second bathing suit, because the one she had used this morning was still wet. Then she walked into the kitchen, got a big jug of water out of the fridge and grabbed a couple of cereal bars.

"I brought some water and snacks too," she said out of breath, as she arrived back at the pick-up.

"Great idea."

And off they went. The road "past" Hana seemed even a bit more challenging than the road to Hana. Sometimes it was extremely steep and narrow and turned into just one lane that wasn't even paved. Sometimes the rusty guardrails looked like someone had crashed into them or there were none at all. Lani was glad that they were driving on the right side of the road, which meant they were driving on the inside and the cars passing them were on the ocean side… And, it was a bit different driving with a local than driving herself.

Max was quite experienced on this road and, in Lani's opinion, he was driving about twice as fast as he should be going. It was white-knuckle driving again, but Lani was the one who had the white knuckles from hanging on to the handle above her door.

"Ummm…" she started, "could you stop driving so crazy?"
But instead of slowing down, he actually drove across to the other side of the road and stopped abruptly in a little parking lot. They had just driven around a very sharp curve with a big roaring waterfall on the right. At first, Lani thought he was upset that she had called his driving crazy, but he simply ignored what she had said.

"Come on, I want you to meet my friend Laura and see Wailua Falls!"
A middle-aged artist with curly gray hair had set up a stand on the side of the small parking lot where she was selling beautiful tropical prints. Max introduced them.

"Hey, Laura, I want you to meet my friend Lani. She is staying at Koki Beach House. Lani, this is Laura Cattleya. Which, of course, is not her real name," he said with a grin.

"Hi, Lani!" said Laura who had at first only stolen a quick glance at Lani, but then she had to look again.
Lani answered: "Hi, how are you? I love your paintings."

"Thank you!" Laura couldn't stop looking at Lani. "Wow, you look really familiar. Are you from here?"

"It's funny that you should mention that," mentioned Max. "That's exactly what we're trying to figure out."
"Well, I must be from here somehow. I never met my parents. I was adopted and live in the Hudson Valley, in Upstate New York. But out of the blue I got this letter a few weeks ago, saying that I inherited Koki Beach House. I'm still in shock, and now there is this incredible painting of a woman in the house who looks exactly like me."
Laura looked at Max, then at Lani.

"Wow! That's quite the story. Yes, that's why you look familiar. There are quite a few of those paintings. They're by a painter named Paul Kent. He used to come here all the time to paint, but then his mother got really sick and he couldn't come for a few years. The story is that the girl in the painting is Luana Kalekilio."

"Kalekilio?" asked Lani. "Isn't that the name of the people who run the Island General Store?" She looked at Max who was squirming and felt very uncomfortable that he hadn't told her more yet.

Laura continued. "Yes, she was their daughter who suddenly disappeared from the face of the Earth one day."
She looked at Lani.

"You look exactly like Luana. It's unbelievable. Maybe it's true that she had a child after all. People gossiped that she was pregnant when she disappeared, but nobody ever knew for sure…" she said, immersed in her memories.

"Paul used to stay in a cabin right up the road, close to Waioka Pond. We met a few times briefly. Very nice guy. The cabin is old and abandoned now, but I think it's still there. Painters used to stay there all the time, because it was set up like a perfect little studio and it had a really romantic view. You should go and check it out," she said to Lani. Now she looked at Max, giving him directions. "Park as if you're going go Waioka Pond, climb through the same gate and walk across the meadow as if you're going to the pool, but instead of taking the right to Waioka Pond, you continue straight towards the ocean… then you walk left across the meadow until you get to a little wooded area. Walk through that and you'll come right up to the little cabin. It's grayish blue and overlooks the ocean. I'm not sure if it's safe to go inside, it's probably been abandoned for over twenty years now."

Chapter 22

They thanked Laura Cattleya, got back into the pick-up and actually had to drive back a couple of miles. They had already driven past Waioka Pond. Max had gotten the hint and drove much slower now. They were both quite silent. Lani's brain was full of new information. The popular daughter of the local grocery store owners suddenly disappears one day, and people didn't even know if she had really been pregnant, or not. Was that her mother? But it must have been her, since she looked exactly like her. Was that the reason the grocery store owner had looked at her like that? And that she felt this weird connection? He'd be her grandfather. And then the painter Paul Kent, who painted the girl so many times. Was he Lani's father and where was he now? Max felt quite awful, because he hadn't found the right time to tell Lani about the feud between Malani Kahale and her brother Kumu Kalekilio and that maybe for that reason, Malani had left the house to Lani and not to her brother.

Max stopped on a straight stretch of road that looked like cars parked there frequently. It was fenced in on the ocean side.

"Take your bathing suit," he said. "Just in case. While we're here, we can go swimming in Waioka Pond on the way back."

She grabbed her little backpack. They passed a little honor system fruit stand, had to jump over the guard rail and then climb through the metal beams of a big cattle gate.

There was a little path leading across a meadow toward the ocean, leading to Waioka Pond on the right. Max and Lani continued walking straight and turned left where Laura had instructed them to go. Now they were walking along a cliff with quite stunning views out onto the ocean. They passed through a patch of trees and arrived in a clearing with the little grayish-blue cabin in the back. It was very small and didn't have more than a studio, a kitchen and little bathroom in it. Max carefully opened the door which he had to give quite a hard push and that squeaked very loudly into the silence and made both of them look at each other with big wide eyes. They felt a bit like burglars since this was all private property. We could see dust particles flying in the light coming in from a big oceanfront window with years of dirt and dust on it. An old easel still stood at the window, and we could envision a painter standing there, painting exactly the breathtaking view that we saw right now. They both looked around, trying to find something that Paul Kent or someone else might have left there. There were some old receipts scattered about on the kitchen counter, but they were not legible and only looked like grocery store and gas station receipts. On the back wall of the studio was an old wooden bed with a nightstand. Lani opened the drawer of the nightstand and stirred up so much dust that she had to cough. Max walked over to a window and forced it open. They needed some fresh air in here. Lani found an old yellowed business card in the drawer: Lisa Holmquist, Art Gallery Lanai, Phone: 808-241-21. Lani didn't know if this was any information that would get her anywhere, but she slid the card into a side pocket of her beachbag that was hanging from her shoulder. That was all there was in the little cabin. Lani looked around again and Max watched her silently. He was enchanted by her classic beauty again. Now was the time that he had to tell her what he knew about the feud between Malani and Kumu.

They quietly left the cabin, walked through the woods and across the meadow and continued straight down a short, rocky path leading toward Waioka Pond, also known as Venus Pool. They walked underneath some trees, then they stood in an open canyon of old lava rock that had been smoothed in millions of years: giant boulders leading down to a protected sparkling blue pool that led into the ocean. The rugged scenery surrounding the area was absolutely stunning. Lani was speechless. From where they were standing, it was about 30 feet straight down to the water.

"You can jump in from right here. It's awesome!" said Max.

He pulled his shirt off and stood there, just in his bathing suit. Then he jumped forward and plunged the thirty feet down and disappeared in the water, to come up a few seconds later that seemed like an eternity for Lani. She was horrified.

"Wow!" Max shouted from below, shaking his head to get the water out of his ears. "The water's great! Jump in!" he yelled up at Lani.

"Never!" yelled Lani and laughed, relieved that he was okay. While Max was still swimming in the water thirty feet below her, Lani quickly used the opportunity to change into her bathing suit. She would never jump from where she was, but she climbed a bit more than halfway down and then did the exhilarating jump. She plunged down into the deep refreshing water and surfaced, gasping for air. Then she swam to the other side of the pool where Max was pounding a coconut against a rock. He knew exactly how to hit it to crack it just at the top. He handed the coconut to Lani and made motions for her to drink the water. She took it, tilted her head back and held the coconut up and the warm coconut water poured into her mouth. Then Max took it back, hit it against the rock with a few more blows, pulled the shell apart and handed her a few pieces of juicy fresh coconut meat.

They just sat there, chewing for a while, looking at the roaring ocean past the pool and then he started telling her what he knew...

"Well, I'm sorry that I haven't told you this earlier, but I think with all this new information we're uncovering, I have to tell you about the situation in town that might have to do with you too... Unfortunately, it's not very pleasant..."

She perked her ears. She had so many questions and everyone only seemed to be telling her bits and pieces of the story.

"I only know what I was told, because all of this happened when I was a little kid. I don't think I'm much older than you... There was a really bad fight between Kumu Kalekilio and his daughter when she was eighteen and about to start her senior year in high school, and one night she disappeared from the face of the Earth. Some people say she was pregnant and he wanted to talk her into having an abortion, because this baby was from a Haole. That's what white people are called here. But nobody knows for sure whether she was really pregnant or not. The Kalekilios kept it a secret."

Lani's jaw dropped. So the nice old man at the Island General Store had not wanted her.

Max continued. "As I just said, nobody knows if she was even pregnant. Kumu accused his sister Malani of helping Luana run away, or he blamed her that Luana left, but she insisted she had nothing to do with it … and they never spoke again. For thirty years."

"The entire town has been split up into the people on Kumu's side and the people on Malani's side. The ones against Haoles, who think the white man just comes here and takes what he wants, the other more tolerant ones who think that Kumu should have supported his daughter, no matter what, because it's family that counts. It's so bad, that people like me, who were on Malani's side, haven't shopped at the Island General Store for thirty years."

"The police searched for Luana for years and there were signs all over Maui, but she was never found. That's basically all I know. But it looks like she did have a daughter, and that's you…"

"…Oh, and when Malani died, everyone thought that Kumu and his wife would inherit Koki Beach House, since they are her last living relatives… And now you came along…"

Lani swallowed hard. "So, I'm probably not very popular here right now, just coming along and taking away what they think belongs to them…Wow! What a situation! No wonder you didn't want to tell me. I'm not so sure what to do myself…"

Her head was spinning and he could tell that she was overwhelmed with all this information. They just sat there quietly, until she shook off the gloomy feelings for now and stood up.

"I'll deal with that later," she said and jumped back into the water. He jumped in as well and they swam, racing back to the other side of the pool, while he slowed down a bit to let her win…

It was getting late. They had to change back into dry clothes, which they did shyly, pretending not to look at each other while they took their wet bathing suits off, but secretly catching a curious glimpse of each other. Then they packed up their things and hiked back to the car.

They continued their venture on the "Road Past Hana", past Wailua Falls again, honked briefly and waved at Laura Cattleya, who waved back, smiling happily. They crossed a bridge where Max briefly stopped and showed her 'O'he'o Gulch.

"People falsely call it the Seven Sacred Pools which it was just named for marketing purposes. We don't have enough time to stop here today, but it's probably closed anyway, since it's been raining a lot. There can be flash floods here coming down from the mountains, which are quite dangerous."

Max accelerated again. Lani looked at him with wide eyes again, so he grinned and slowed down a bit. Right before the left turn to the church with Charles Lindbergh's grave, he stopped at a Thai food truck that was parked in the grass behind a rusty old fifties truck that was almost fully overgrown by lilikoi vine. The roof and hood were covered with sticky rotting fruit. They walked up to the food truck, started chatting with the owner and Lani told the middle-aged Hawaiian woman, Pekelo, her story. Again, just like with Laura Cattleya, there was something about this woman that Lani felt compelled to tell her everything without even knowing her… Pekelo looked up, froze and stared at Lani for a few seconds and, even though she was too young to know Luana Kalekilio, she remembered the flyers that had hung all over the island years later.

"My grandmother is an old Hawaiian healer, a Kahuna. She might know something about your mother. She went to see a friend today though and isn't here. Can you come back tomorrow? You should definitely talk to her."

Lani looked at Max. He said: "I have to work tomorrow, but I guess you can come back by yourself?"

"Yeah, I'd love to come back and talk to her. When's a good time?"

"She usually rests after lunch. How about late morning?"

"Sure. Thanks."

Max ordered a few dishes to go and Pekelo packed the food up and put it in a big brown paper bag. She also gave them some samples of a new dish she had cooked for the first time today and some chicken satay. It was delicious. That's when they both realized how hungry they were and wondered if they should eat their food right away, but Pekelo's samples were so big that they were good for now. She also gave them some delicious Thai tea, which was quite filling.

It was almost dark when they arrived back at Koki Beach House. They warmed up the Thai food and had dinner on the porch, while they seemed to have endless subjects to talk about. He finally shyly said good night and got up and left.

"Oh, and if you want to go swimming in the morning, please let me know! I'll be there. It's better to have a buddy in that water."

She nodded thankfully. "Thanks. Good night."

Chapter 23

Lani laid awake for a long time, listening to the roaring waves crashing against the rocks, thinking about Max, Kumu and the other people she had met today. Hana seemed like a small village. Everyone knew everyone and there was a lot of gossip. And then Paul Kent. She was wide awake again. She had almost forgotten, since there had been no reception on the road. She sat back up, turned the light on and entered his name into the search engine of her phone:

Countless beautiful images came up, of some of the paintings that she had already seen or others, similar to those. Some of them were his tropical paintings from his time in Hawaii and some were beautiful images of the 1000 Islands in upstate New York. He had been exhibited in the Metropolitan Museum of Art, and there was even a Paul Kent gallery in Clayton in the heart of the 1000 Islands region in New York State and he had held various exhibitions in prestigious galleries in Manhattan. Wow. She had to go there as soon as she was back in New York. Then she read his bio:

"Paul Kent Jr., 1965 – 2005, contemporary fine artist, born in 1965 in Clayton, New York, died in 2005 in Maui, cause of death unknown." She swallowed hard. Wow. Died in Maui. Cause of death unknown. She continued reading.

"Son of Paul Kent Sr., 1936 – 2011, and Bridgett Kent, (Warner), born in 1942. Known for his tropical paintings of Maui, often compared to the style of Georgia O'Keeffe's Maui period, but also realistic portraits and paintings of the 1000 Islands. Professor of Fine Arts at Syracuse Art Institute from 2000 – 2005." That was it. Every other Internet entry just talked about his art and said "cause of death unknown". What had happened to him? And did she still have a grandmother somewhere, since there was no death year for Paul Kent's mother? Now she really couldn't sleep. Her jet lag didn't help either. She tossed and turned until the early morning hours.

The next morning, she had a hard time getting up and had just rolled out of bed and put on her bathrobe when Max knocked at the door. She opened the door.

"Oh, I guess you're not going swimming this morning?" he asked with a smile. "I'm glad you're getting some rest. You've had a few busy days."

"Yeah," she replied. "I couldn't sleep all night. I googled my father, and it's really mysterious…"

Max nodded. "I actually did too. Strange that he died so young and his death happened in Maui, but the cause of death is unknown…"
"Maybe I'll find some more information about him… but maybe I'll never find out. Who knows…" she said sadly.

"Maybe the healer will have some information today." Max replied. "Good luck today. And drive carefully. As long as you drive defensively, you'll be fine. If anyone starts tailgating you, just pull over and let them pass."

"Okay. I'll be fine. Have a nice day."
He turned around, walked down the driveway and took a left toward the beach.

Chapter 24

Lani closed the door, made herself some of the Maui Coffee. Her thoughts were immediately back at Max. She found him quite sexy… It was amazing how well they got along… she smiled while she got up and put the few dishes that she had used into the sink and then packed her backpack and grabbed her purse and a bottle of water for the road.

She drove the same road that she and Max had taken yesterday, but she was definitely slower. It was a big difference to be the driver, because she couldn't admire the views like she had yesterday, because she had to have her eyes riveted on the road, but she stopped a few times when she saw something that she really wanted to see. She drove past Haleakala National Park with 'O'he'o Gulch and the bamboo forest and continued a few more miles to the Thai food truck. Pekelo was puttering around in her food truck, already expecting her.
She looked up and said cheerfully. "Good morning!"

"Good morning," replied Lani.

"My grandmother is a bit tired today after her visit yesterday. She doesn't go out much, but her friend wasn't doing well yesterday and she had to go and see her. She's like a doctor for the older people around here. She's known as a Kahuna, a Hawaiian healer. She was involved in developing a new system of healing based on the ancient spiritual tradition, Ho'oponopono. She's in great health, but she's 95 years old and has become quite frail in the past two years. She's looking forward to meeting you."

Pekelo led her to a very old Polynesian woman, sitting in a beautiful garden – she looked like she was meditating. She had long white hair and wore a haku … a tropical Hawaiian flower crown… on her head. Her dark skin was very wrinkly, but her eyes looked like they were still as sharp as a hawk. She was wearing a long wide flowery mu'umu'u and open-toed sandals.

"Tutu," Pekelo began, "This is the young woman I told you about who is looking for her mother."

"Lani, this is my grandmother Ana Kamealoha, we all call her Tutu, which means grandmother." Pekelo said to Lani. "I have to get back to the food truck. I'm expecting a busload of customers today."
Lani nodded and thanked her.

Tutu looked at Lani with her kind wise eyes. Without saying a word, she stood up slowly and walked carefully toward her. She was tiny, almost a head smaller than Lani. She took both of Lani's hands in her hands and looked up at her. She had tears in her eyes and caressed Lani's cheek with her hand.

"It's just like Luana has returned," she said with a husky voice. "You look exactly like her, my child. Except your skin is a bit lighter. You are so beautiful."

"Thank you," whispered Lani. She felt very much in awe of this old healer who must have seen so many things in her long life and she felt like she could trust her unconditionally.

"Sit down by the fire with me, wahine nani, beautiful Hawaiian girl." They both walked over to a fire pit in which black lava rocks were smoldering and sat down across from each other. Lani watched her carefully, respectfully. Tutu closed her eyes and chanted something in Hawaiian. Then she continued in English, because she was now speaking to Lani.

"Lava stone is a grounding stone that strengthens one's connection to Mother Earth. It gives us strength and courage, allowing us stability through times of change. This is a time of change for Hana since one of Hana's daughters has returned. Nobody speaks about what happened back then, because we made one of our daughters leave and didn't help her. We need to speak now and step up to help and we must ask for forgiveness: Ho'oponopono", she said in her husky deep voice. "I can see that Luana was in Lanai. She doesn't seem to be there now, but she was there in the past. You must go there and try to find out what happened."

Even though Kumu Kalekilio had indeed, thirty years ago, asked Tutu for herbs to abort the child, her philosophy allowed no judgment or negativity. So, she did not broach this subject that would drive a possibly even deeper wedge between Kumu and Lani. She refused to give him any herbs back then, because in her opinion, it was the mother's choice to decide what to do and Luana didn't want an abortion, as far as she was told.

Tutu opened her eyes. She was finished. She made an impression as if all her strength had been sucked out of her and seemed very weak now. She spoke very quietly.

"Go to Lanai and see what you can find, my child. It has changed a lot since then, but you will have the intuition to find the right path. You have my blessings."

Lani was a bit disappointed for a second, but she didn't show it. Lanai was an entire island. How would she know where and what to look for? But she thanked her, got up and said goodbye. She went back to the food truck where Pekelo was busy chopping vegetables in the back. She turned around and handed Lani one of the spring rolls that were lying on several baking sheets, cooling off.

"How did it go?" asked Pekelo.

"Hmmm. She told me to go to Lanai, because she sees that my mother must have been there. But she had no other hints or ideas. Lanai is a whole island. I have no idea where to start."

"The populated areas of Lanai aren't that big. You'll be able to get around and ask people questions pretty quickly. It's kind of like a small town, like Hana, if she is or was there, people will know." said Pekelo. Lani became a little more optimistic again.

"Sounds good. Thanks for all your help. And, by the way, the food yesterday was great." Lani said with a smile and a wave goodbye. She drove back, thinking more about what Tutu had told her and was already planning a trip to Lanai in her mind. This probably meant that she'd have to go all the way back to the West side of Maui to get there.

Chapter 25

When she was back in at Koki Beach House in the mid afternoon, Lani decided that she had to go and see Maui Exotics, the local nursery that carried orchids and tropical flowers, just to see what they had and how a nursery in Hawaii compared to hers at home. It was a very well kept nursery and they had a very nice collection of orchids, but to Lani's big surprise, they didn't have many more orchids than she had in her little nursery in the Hudson Valley. Although she did have to admit that she was quite an obsessive collector and therefore had quite an extensive collection... This nursery seemed to specialize more in tropical flower arrangements with various types of heliconia, ginger and other flowers with big waxy leaves. Phillip Bancroft, the owner, was from England, but had lived here for more than thirty years. He had also known Luana and immediately saw the striking resemblance.

"You must be her daughter. You can't deny it."

"Yes, everybody says that. Too bad there is no trace of her so that I will never know for sure."

"She was very interested in orchids as well, you know, she used to come and work in the greenhouse sometimes after school, and she really loved them."

"Wow, I could have inherited that from her," replied Lani.
When she left, he gave her a beautiful blooming Cattleya as a gift.

"I hope you find more information about your mom. And I also hope that you decide to stay and renovate the house. So, this could be your first orchid of a new collection in Maui. I always think of expanding the nursery, I could use a partner or additional employee..."

"Awww, thank you very much. You never know! It was so nice to meet you, Phillip!"

On the way back to the house, she made a detour and drove past the Island General Store, she couldn't stand the situation with her grandparents any longer and stopped and parked. She was determined to walk inside the store and confront her grandfather and grandmother or at least go and see them. She walked up to the store's front door. Through the glass, she saw a friendly older lady at the cash register, talking to a customer. The old man, who obviously was Kumu Kalekilio, stepped up and made some waving motions toward the door, obviously explaining something or giving directions. All three people stopped talking, when they discovered Lani standing behind the glass, watching them. She stepped back quickly, turned around, walked quickly back to her car and drove away.

She just didn't know what to say to them. Why did you make my mother leave?

Why did you not want me? She felt like a little child just running away like that, but couldn't help it.

Kumu and Leila Kalekilio both walked slowly to the door and watched Lani drive away. They were even more embarrassed than she was. They wanted to meet their granddaughter badly, who looked exactly like their daughter thirty years ago, and they wanted her to forgive them, but didn't know how to go about contacting her. The feeling of guilt was too big and the whole situation was so awkward. On the outside they seemed friendly toward customers and the people in town, but deep in their hearts, Mr. and Mrs. Kalekilio had turned into bitter old people, due to what they had done to their own daughter and the guilt that was eating away at them from the inside.

Chapter 26

Just as Lani pulled into the driveway of Koki Beach House, Max came walking up from the beach, a surfboard under his arm. His wet black curly hair was glistening in the sun, and all he was wearing was a bathing suit. He was still wet and hadn't even bothered bringing a towel. She soaked up the sight of his muscular tanned body and couldn't take her eyes off of him. She jumped out of the car as he came walking up.

"Wow, I didn't know you surf! I'd love to check that out. Do you think you could teach me?"

"Sure. I'll see if I can borrow a second surfboard somewhere. How was your day?"

"I went and saw Tutu, the old healer."
He stopped in front of her. "And what did she say?"

"I have to go to Lanai. She saw that my mother was there and told me to go and find out what might have happened."

"Well, that's quite a trip." He thought for a second, then he continued: "You have to go all the way to Lahaina and take a ferry from there, which usually leaves in the morning. So, you would probably have to stay in Lahaina the night before and then again in Lahaina or Paia the night after, if you want a full day in Lanai and don't want to drive back to Hana too exhausted..."

"I need to go as soon as possible. Otherwise, it'll drive me crazy."

"Don't forget that my handyman friends are stopping by tomorrow. I'm off for three days Friday, Saturday and Sunday, if you'd like me to go with you."
She was thankful and smiled. He knew his way around much better and she wouldn't mind spending some more time with him...

"Thank you. That would be great."

"Okay, I have friends who own an Italian restaurant in Lahaina. They have a big condo with a guestroom that we might be able to stay in. I'll call them and ask if we can stay there Friday night."

"Awesome."

"Do you have plans tonight?" Max asked spontaneously.

"Not really. I was just going to hang out."

"There's a Jazz combo playing at the Hana Hotel tonight. Do you wanna go? The musicians are friends of mine. And something like this is a big deal in sleepy Hana. There's usually not much going on," he said with a grin.

She grinned back. "Jazz Combo? That doesn't sound very Hawaiian."

"Well, I guess there are enough Hawaiian bands around. They thought there would be a market for Jazz in upscale hotels, and they actually get quite a lot of gigs at the nicer hotels all around the islands, especially in Honolulu. You could call it Hawaiian Jazz. The drummer is from Hana, that's why they're playing here for two nights. Tomorrow they're playing at his father's 60th birthday party."

Lani nodded. "I'd love to go. It sounds like fun."

"We could go and have drinks and a couple of appetizers first. Nobody can really afford a whole dinner there," he said and grinned again. She noticed a dimple in his chin, which made her heart flutter a little.

"Yeah, it seems quite pricey," she replied, a bit distracted.

"Can you be ready by seven?" he asked.

She looked at her phone. It was 6:30. Half an hour was plenty of time for her to get ready.

"Sure."

"Okay. See you in a bit."

She nodded and walked over to the house.

Or maybe half an hour wasn't plenty of time after all. She looked at the selection of clothes she had brought and became a bit nervous. After all, this felt a little like a real date with a really cute guy. She had a ton of casual sundresses and a ton of shorts and skorts and t-shirts, but Hana Hotel was quite an upscale hotel. She had a more formal dress and a skirt and blouse that she had brought for her appointment with Pike Kahananui, but they almost seemed too conservative for a date with Max. She tried on several outfits, but nothing looked acceptable. Finally, at about five minutes to seven, she stood in front of the full-length mirror and turned satisfied back and forth. She was wearing her formal skirt, but had matched it with a casual gypsy blouse and a colorful scarf around her waist. One of the pairs of sandals she had brought had dark brown chunky two-inch heals. They looked great with the skirt and her long legs appeared even longer than they were. Her long dark straight hair was freshly brushed and shiny and her make-up was minimal with some mascara, powder and lip-gloss, but made a big difference, since she usually didn't wear any make-up. She rushed downstairs, grabbed her purse and in that exact instance, Max knocked at the door.

He looked quite stylish himself, compared to his usual faded jeans or board shorts. He was wearing a pair of khakis, a nice vintage Hawaii shirt with a print of surfing hula girls on it and brown loafers. When he saw Lani, he was more than pleased with what he saw.

"You look incredible," he said quietly, admiring the lovely woman in front of him.

"Thanks. You don't look so bad yourself," she replied and grinned.

They walked to the pick-up truck and were on their way.

Chapter 27

The band had already started playing when they entered the crowded bar of the Hana Hotel. The musicians were set up on a little stage on the opposite side of the bar. A keyboard player, bassist and a drummer, accompanied by a stunning female singer, with short platinum blonde hair, currently singing "The girl from Ipanema" with a smoky, sexy voice. They sounded very good. Max's jaw dropped when he saw the singer, but Lani's jaw dropped even more when the band had finished the song, the singer immediately made her way straight through the crowd toward Max, hugged him tightly and gave him a kiss on the lips.

"Maxi! It's so good to see you! I hope you have some time for me while I'm here!"

"Ummm." He looked at Lani from the side and introduced them. "Lani, this is Mandy, Mandy, this is my friend Lani..."

"Hi." "Hi." They both said simultaneously with chilly voices. If looks could kill, both of the two women would have dropped dead right now.

"Well, nice to see you both." Mandy said quickly. "I have to get back on stage. Why don't you stay for a drink after the show, Maxiiii?" she said, looking at Max, batting her fake eyelashes while extending the "i' in Maxi a bit too long. It was like a fingernail scratching on a chalkboard for Lani.

Lani was really bummed. She had thought Max was this nice shy guy who couldn't harm a fly and now he seemed to be going out with her while he still had this old flame, or maybe even worse, an existing relationship? He also seemed to know every single good-looking woman in this place, although, in fairness to him, Lani knew Hana was a small village and everybody knew each other.

They were lucky to be able to grab one of the small round hightops at the bar, although they both would have rather gone home immediately.

"I'm sorry. I had no idea she was going to be here. Mandy used to tour with them, but started working fulltime in a bar in Honolulu two years ago and was replaced by a new singer. She's a bit crazy. We've never had a relationship, but she acted almost like a stalker when she performed here the last time."

"Okay…" replied Lani, subdued.

"Let's just eat something and get out of here," said Max. "I can say hi to my buddies tomorrow."

Yeah, and to Mandy, while I'm not there, Lani thought… but she quickly shook those feelings of jealousy off and decided not to let the crazy singer ruin her evening, and the band did sound quite good.

They ordered cocktails and some appetizers and enjoyed the music, food and drinks.

Something popped up in Lani's mind. "By the way, do you know Pineapple Peter? I stopped there on my drive here, and he seemed to know my mother too. It was so awkward. He just stared at me and I didn't know what to say."

Max nodded. "As a matter of fact, I do know Peter, he's a great guy. He used to live in Hana and I'm friendly with his little brother Aaron. Aaron is a great artist and owns a gallery in Paia now. You should also take a look at the gallery here in the hotel. They carry some of his paintings and other great artwork."

She perked her ears, full of interest.

"If you want, we can go for a walk over there now. I think it's open in the evening."

Max was eager to leave the bar. He didn't feel comfortable with Mandy being there and constantly looking over at them. They had had a very brief fling a few years ago and she had turned out to be quite crazy. He wanted to spare Lani any further details…

"Yeah, let's go. I don't feel comfortable with that crazy singer constantly staring at us anyway," she replied and they both had to laugh about her honesty.

"Same," he answered.

While they walked out, Lani noticed an older man who had been staring at her the entire evening. She nudged Max's side slightly and said to him: "Speaking of people staring. Do you happen to know that guy over there? He's been staring at me the whole evening…"

"Yeah. I don't like that guy. He stays here from time to time and seems to be trying to buy some of the oceanfront properties. He acts as if he owns the place. He's an investor who would probably like to bulldoze the entire coast and build highrises instead. His name is Joseph McAllen."

"He's been staring at me in an almost creepy manner."

"Yeah, that's strange. I don't know. Maybe he recognizes you too from one of the paintings? Or maybe he wants to buy Koki Beach House and knows you live there..."

"That's true."

She shuddered and tried to forget about the man.

It was a short walk to the gallery across a courtyard with a pretty big water fountain in the center and big blooming plumeria trees. It was a balmy starry night with the new moon high up in the sky. Cicadas were chirping noisily and the ocean was roaring in the distance. They both felt the romantic atmosphere and were electrified when their hands brushed against each other while they were walking. They both glanced at each other out of the corner of their eyes, their hearts beating...

All of the doors leading into the gallery were open on this beautiful night and they stepped inside and were surrounded by beautiful jewelry and artwork. A middle-aged Hawaiian woman greeted them. Every time Lani saw a middle-aged person now, she almost expected them to say something about Luana, but this time the lady didn't say anything. She was hesitant. She looked down.

"Alana, this is Lani. I think Billy told you about her. He's coming over to Koki Beach House to do an estimate on some repairs tomorrow.

"Lani, this is Alana, Billy's wife."

Alana came around the counter and walked over toward Lani. Without a word, she took her in her arms. She had tears in her eyes.

"I was your mother's best friend," she explained.

Lani and Max looked at each other, full of surprise. Wow, thought Lani, I found my mother's best friend. That's amazing.

Alana continued: "I drove her to the harbor in Lahaina the day she snuck out of her parent's house, where she took the ferry to Lanai. Malani had arranged for everything."

"Do you know where she stayed in Lanai?"

"No. I'm so sorry. I wish I had more information for you. Malani and Luana purposely didn't give me any information about Luana's destination, because Malani and Luana were so afraid that her parents or someone else would find her. Even the fact that I knew she was going to Lanai was risky. Luana's parents and even the police could have questioned me. But they didn't know that I took her to the ferry. I never told anyone. I never saw or heard from her again. It still breaks my heart. But I'm happy to see you and that you look like you're doing well. I know everyone probably says this to you, but you do look like her mirror image. I feel like I've gone back in time, seeing you stand here like this."

Lani looked at Max. It was late and he had to work tomorrow and it was probably boring for him to have to listen to this conversation.

"Would you mind if I came back tomorrow? I'd love to come and take a closer look at the gallery too. It's late," she nodded toward Max.

"Don't forget that Billy and Keanu are coming over tomorrow," Max reminded her. "But it shouldn't take too long."

"They're coming over at 9:30, aren't they?" Lani looked at Alana and asked her: "Will you be around after lunch?"

Alana replied: "Would you like to have lunch together? My treat. I get a discount at the hotel."

"I'd love to have lunch with you," replied Lani. "Is 12:30 okay for tomorrow?"

"Yes, I'll see you tomorrow. Bye, Max. It was good to see you both."

"Good night, Alana."

Both Lani and Max were quite silent during the quick drive home. The atmosphere was extremely romantic, the moonlight sparkled on the ocean as they passed Koki beach with Alau Island that looked like a giant shark's fin sticking out of the ocean in the distance. There was tension in the car, Max just wanted to stop the car, take her in his arms and kiss her, but Lani seemed to be somewhere else with her thoughts…

As soon as they turned into the driveway of Koki Beach House and Max slowed down to park the car, Lani gathered all her courage and asked the question Max wasn't expecting at all:

"So, were you and Mandy ever a couple?"

"Hmmm... not really. She and the combo had a longer gig at the hotel and I hung out there quite often. We both got pretty drunk one night and ended up having a one-night stand. I think she was hoping for more, but I had just ended a long-term relationship and was never in love with her."

Lani looked straight ahead, hiding any emotions.

"I'm not too proud of what happened." said Max. "And then she wouldn't stop calling me even though I told her to back off... she is seriously a bit crazy... and then thankfully their gig in Hana ended and they started touring in Oahu. She kept calling me for a while, but I ended up not answering my phone anymore, and she finally got the hint... I had no idea she'd be here tonight. Their new singer must be sick or something. I know they're very happy with the other girl. I'm really sorry, the fact that Mandy was there kinda put a damper on the evening. If I had known, I never would have asked you to go."

Lani was overwhelmed and tired. She just nodded, got out of the car, said quickly: "It's not your fault, I guess. Good night," and disappeared in the house.

He just sat there for a while, wondering what he had done wrong, after being so honest with her. Maybe too honest, he thought to himself.

Chapter 28

They both tossed and turned all night, thinking of each other and wondering if the other had the same feelings, but finally both fell into a deep dreamless sleep in their lonely beds.

The next morning, Lani woke up, feeling exhausted. She was relieved that she had no other plans than the two handymen coming over and then going to have lunch with Alana. She was about to make her obligatory phone calls to the nursery and her parents, when suddenly someone knocked at the door. It was Max, in a swimsuit and rash guard.

"I found a second surfboard. Do you want to have a lesson this morning?" he asked with a smile.

It was hard to turn down that smile, especially since she had always wanted to learn surfing. When you're in Hawaii, you have to go surfing. And they still had two hours before the two handymen were coming over. She nodded, smiling.

"Let me go and put on my bathing suit!" she replied upbeat. "How about a coffee while you wait?"

"Sure." He stepped inside the house and walked toward the kitchen, while she walked into the bedroom to change quickly. The incident with Mandy yesterday seemed forgotten. When she came out of the bedroom in her swimsuit and a terry cloth dress, he was already standing at the entrance with two coffees to go. He handed one to her.

"Wow! Great service!" she mentioned with a smile. They each grabbed one of the surfboards leaning against the garage door and were off to the two minute walk down to Hamoa Beach, Lani had her beachbag hanging from her shoulder, both of them under one arm a surfboard and in the other hand a coffee.

The sun had just gone up a while ago and was still low in the sky, making the light at Hamoa Beach soft and diffused. The waves were nice and gentle this morning, perfect for a beginner.

First, Max showed Lani in the sand how to get up on the board.

"You're lying on the board, place your hands on the side of the board a bit lower than your shoulders, slightly raise your chest, jump up quickly sideways, with your knees slightly bent, with the left leg in the front and the right in the back. The momentum of the wave will take you to shore while you try to keep your balance."
They practiced a few times in the sand.

"Okay, first fasten the tether around your ankle and let's go into the water and practice paddling a little," Max said.

They walked toward the water, pushed the surfboards past the small wavebreak, then they jumped onto the surfboards with their chest down and both arms paddling.

"Cup your hands and use big long strokes. The nose of the board should just be sticking out of the water, scoot a bit back, you're a bit too far in the front," yelled Max against the roaring ocean. Lani followed his example. They turned the surfboards around, now facing the beach and sat there, waiting for a wave. Right before Max started feeling the momentum of the wave which was approaching quickly, he made a signal for her to start paddling as hard as she could and then to get up as she had practiced in the sand. She was about to jump up, when the wave hit her from the side, she lost her balance and tumbled head first into the water. All she felt was that she was being spun around by the wave. She swam up from under water, gasping for air, while she felt the surfboard pulling at her ankle. Thank goodness she had the tether and therefore was able to regain control over the board and hang on to it, while the next wave was already coming up. It washed over her, but basically the water was already so shallow that she felt the sand under her feet. She jumped on the board anyway and paddled the few feet and let the tiny waves wash her ashore.

Laughing, she laid in the sand, looking up at Max who had followed the whole thing and came to check whether she was okay. He saw that she was laughing and smiled.

"Well, that was quite clumsy, but fun," she said laughing.

"Haha, you did good! You can't expect to stand up the very first time! Try again!" he replied and walked ahead into the water, pushing his board. As soon as he came up to the first break, he jumped onto his surfboard and dove through the wave. She tried the same thing and it worked! She was past the wavebreak and could now just float on the board and relax. They just hung out on their surfboards out there for a while, but then Max saw the perfect wave approaching, made signs for her to start paddling as hard as she could and then, as soon as she felt the momentum of the wave pushing her, to stand up. This time she did and she felt the accelerating feeling of the wave pushing her ashore, while she stood on her board, crouched down a little, holding her balance. She stood all the way, correcting her posture, until the current pushed her board all the way into the sand.

"Haha," she laughed. "That was so much fun! I was so slow in the end, I'm sure it looked comical!"

"No, you did great," Max replied who had also reached the beach with his board. He walked up to her and gave her a high-five. "You're a natural! That was only your second attempt! Let's keep practicing, we have a little more time!"

They continued surfing for another twenty minutes and with every wave that Lani caught, she felt more confident, but she also had some hard falls into the water, with water getting up her nose and mouth. Thankfully, the ocean was very kind and mild this morning and not as wild and stormy as it could be sometimes. They had a great time, laughed happily when they caught a wave together and high-fived when they arrived together on the beach. After a while, Max pointed at his watch.

"It's 8:45. We should get going, to be ready for the guys at 9:30." Lani was surprised. "Oh, wow, I had no idea it's that late already! Time flies when you're having so much fun!"

They took a quick shower at the fresh water shower, dried off with the towels Lani had brought, grabbed their surfboards and walked the few hundred yards along the street back home.

"What a great feeling to get such a workout first thing in the morning!" exclaimed Lani. "That was fun! Thank you very much for the lesson!"

"My pleasure. You're a real natural. You should keep practicing. I can keep the surfboard for a while," he replied. "I'm going to go and change and have a quick bite to eat. I'm starving. See you at 9:30." With these words, he leaned his surfboard against the building and stepped into the guesthouse.

Chapter 29

Half an hour later, there was a loud knock at the door. Lani opened. It was Max, Keanu and Billy. Keanu and Billy had driven together and knocked at Max's door first, because they knew he was keeping an eye on the renovations for Lani and Pike Kahananui.

"Aloha, guys! Thanks for coming over! Come on in." Lani greeted them.

"Good morning," Keanu and Billy said simultaneously.

"Can I get you guys anything to drink? Coffee, water?" asked Lani. They all shook their heads. "Thanks, maybe later. Let's take a look first."

Max said to Lani: "I wanted to show them the wall in the kitchen first. Where it looks like there's water damage..."

They all walked over to the dining area right behind the kitchen counter, and Max showed the two men the water spots all along the lower wall. They checked the area with their hands and fingers, Keanu got a little hammer out of one of the pockets of his overalls and hammered the wall a bit: That area basically disintegrated and there was immediately a hole in the wall!

"It looks like some parts of this house were built with single wall construction," said Keanu.

"No drywall, no insulation. And the wet wood has just rotted over time."

"Oh, boy," said Billy and looked at Max and Lani. "This whole wall probably has to be replaced, and if you're going to do it, you want to do it right. That means replacing this simple wall with drywall or two insulated layers. Otherwise, your electric wiring will be exposed like here."

"Well, we might have to do it the cheap way," replied Max and looked at Lani. "I don't know if Lani can afford to go all the way out and spend a fortune on the renovations."

Lani nodded. "Yeah, I'm not sure either. I guess we can look at the two different alternatives and see how much it adds up to?"

Billy nodded. He measured the area and then he measured the entire wall in case everything had to be replaced. He had a notepad and took some notes.

In this instance, Lani's phone rang. She looked at the display. It was Anne in the nursery. "Excuse me, gentlemen, I have to take this call. I'll be right back."

She stepped into her bedroom and closed the door.

As soon as Lani had closed the door, Keanu and Billy started giggling and pointing their fingers at Max like teenage boys, even though they were middle-aged men.

"Haha! I can see that you have a crush on her! So overprotective and the way you look at her! You have love in your eyes!" said Billy and Keanu added: "Max is in love! In lohove…."

Max became upset. He turned around to see if Lani had heard them and shushed his friends. "Stop it, guys! Do you always have to behave like high schoolers?!"

Keanu and Billy just giggled and gently nudged Max in the ribs.

In the meantime, Lani answered the phone with an upbeat voice. "Hey, Anne! How is everything going?"

"Hi, Lani! How is Maui treating you?"

"Well, I hate to tell you that I went surfing this morning and was able to get up!" Lani answered cheerfully. "It was so much fun!"

"That's awesome! Enjoy it!"

"Unfortunately, it's not only fun and games. Right now, I have some handymen here who are taking a look at how much work the house needs. Some things look quite bad. There has been quite some water damage…"

"Oh no, and I'm sorry to say that I have some good news and some bad news too…"

"What's going on? Good news first!"

"The good news is, everything is okay and actually another company, a really nice boutique downtown, signed up for several bouquets per week."

"Wow, that really is good news! Good job, Anne! And the bad news…?"

"Bad news is it's been really cold and there's another really bad cold front coming, and I just opened the power bill, because Bill told me to. He said we have to make sure to keep payments up to date, so that the power doesn't get turned off…"

"Oh no, and how much is it?"

"Twelve hundred dollars," replied Anne.

Wow. Thank goodness, Lani had the money from her parents, but it was slowly dwindling and she had no idea how much she would need for the house, but she didn't want to burden Anne with that news.

"Okay. Thanks for letting me know. I'll make an online payment today. And say thanks to Bill too. I really appreciate you guys taking such good care of things."

"No problem. It's actually been fun so far. He's quite nice."

"I'm sorry, but I have to be short. I have to get back to the handymen."

"Okay, bye, Lani!"

"Bye, Anne! And thanks!"

She opened the door and walked back to join the men, who were in the downstairs bathroom in the meantime, which currently didn't even have water.

Lani asked: So, how bad is it in here?"

Keanu answered: "There's some water damage here too. The pipes have been leaking and some of them need to be replaced. But first we have to take care of the wet spots. We should set up some fans as soon as possible to dry the wall out, otherwise it might get moldy."

Billy took some more notes.

"Can you do that right away?" asked Lani.

"Yes", answered Keanu. A friend of ours in Kahului owns some industrial fans. We can borrow them. We just have to go and get them."

"Hmmm… She looked at Max. They were scheduled to go to Lanai tomorrow and wouldn't be able to go to Kahului and bring the fans back. Max was thinking the same thing. "I'll see if any of my coworkers have to go to Kahului tomorrow or are there already…" he said.

"What else?" asked Billy.

"I'm not sure if we have to do cosmetic things, but the sink and tub in here are totally rusty. They might need to be replaced," answered Max.

„That's not much in the big scheme of things." Billy jotted it down. „What else?"

"The entire roof has to be replaced."

"That will have to be done by a professional roofing company. I can give you some phone numbers of buddies of mine in Kahului. Let's go outside and I'll take a look." said Keanu.
They all walked outside through the front door and looked up at the roof.

"Hmmm… hard to say," continued Keanu. "But I'd guess that it's going to be about fifteen thousand dollars for both the house and the guest house."

"Oh, and the garage door spring is broken. It can't be opened right now," added Max, as he looked at the guesthouse. "And there are some minor things in the guest house. We can look at those later. I want to show you the some of the deck that might have to be replaced. Maybe this time we should use composite instead of wood."

"Although, then you'd have to replace the entire deck," replied Billy. "That might not be necessary."

While they walked from the back of the house toward the guesthouse, Max came up with something else. "When you think about it, the whole house has to be painted too…"
They all looked at the house and nodded. The paint definitely looked old and faded and was flaking off in lots of areas, especially on the guesthouse. Billy took some more notes.
Lani's head was spinning. That was an endless list of repairs. And they hadn't seen the guesthouse yet…
Now they walked into the guesthouse. Even though it was perfectly clean and looked like you could even eat off of the kitchen floor, Max kept apologizing about how messy it was.

"Wow, you should see my house at home," laughed Lani.

Billy and Keanu had to grin. Let's see how this clean freak does with a messy girlfriend, they thought to themselves.

The guesthouse was set up like a studio. There was just a little open kitchenette, a Murphy bed in the living room and a separate bathroom. It was pretty and sunny, with a window front facing the yard and the ocean and even some skylights in the kitchenette's ceiling. Max led them into the kitchen and opened the stove carefully to not break the door off. The flooding had also affected the kitchen on the west side and the south side facing the ocean. Lots of the tile in the kitchen had fallen off and the wall behind them was cracked. Billy opened the cabinets under the stove and sink, kneeled down, pushed some pots aside and felt the bottom and back wall with his hand.

"It feels a bit damp," he said. "That's not a good sign. It might mean that, in addition to the water damage from the storm, there is something wrong with the pipes. Max, we can only guess right now. Eventually, you're going to have to empty all the cabinets, so that we can open the wall..."

Max nodded.

Keanu and Billy measured walls, kitchen appliances and Billy jotted everything down.

"Let's go sit down and try to come up with a list of what's most urgent and what's not so urgent. I'm not sure if we can give you an exact estimate this quickly, Lani. It might take a few days to check on prices for parts and appliances."

"How about some coffee now?" asked Keanu with a smile.

They all realized that they were hungry. Thankfully, Lani had bought some pastries and bread, cheese and deli meat the day before. She went into the kitchen to make coffee, while Max, Billy and Keanu sat down at the table. Billy and Keanu started grinning again, looking at Lani's beautiful figure as she turned around to look into the fridge... Max shook his head and glared at them.

"Let's concentrate, men," he said and carefully tore Billy's notes out of the notepad to be able to look at them while he started a new, updated list.

"So, most urgent is the wet area in the master bathroom," he said and wrote that under point one. "I'm going to call my buddy Sam right now and ask if he happens to be in Kahului. His girlfriend lives there and he's there on most of his days off." He got up and stepped out of the sliding-glass door onto the deck and spoke with his coworker Sam. He was indeed in Kahului, was going back to Hana this afternoon and would be able to bring the fans from Keanu and Billy's friend.

"Awesome. So, we can get started on drying the wall today. It's quite noisy, Lani, but I guess you can turn them off when you go to bed."

"The ocean is so loud," she answered, "that it probably won't even bother me. I love to sleep with the windows open."
She came around the counter and set down a tray with delicious pastries, French bread, sliced ham and cheese, as well as some pineapple and papaya. Then she walked back to the kitchen to grab the coffee, four cups and four plates.

"Help yourselves," she said, while she poured coffee into the cups and handed them to Keanu, Billy and Max.

"Wow, this is great, thanks," said Max.
Keanu and Billy nodded. "Thanks," they said simultaneously.
For a moment we could have heard a pin drop. Everyone was quiet, just enjoying breakfast. After they had satisfied their first hunger, they went down the list of things to do and put them in order, according to urgency. Everything seemed urgent besides the outside paint and the appliances in the bathroom that were more cosmetic.
Keanu and Billy finally got up. Keanu said: "Sorry, it looks like we're going to have to do some research first before we can give you any numbers. But with just the roof being around $15,000, you know you're going to be way up there… It might be close to $100,000." Lani nodded.

She and Max walked them through the front door to the driveway. "Thanks for coming, guys. It was really nice to meet you."

"We'll let Max know as soon as we have some numbers we can work with," replied Keanu.

"Thanks for the coffee and breakfast," said Billy.

While they walked back to the house, Lani asked Max:

"I hope this is not a dumb question, but why did Malani let the house go like this? She can't have been this penniless if she owned a house like this and was able to travel all the time?"

"Good question. But the last few years she was indeed quite penniless. She lost almost all of her money when the stock market crashed. She got tons of offers from real estate developers for the house, but for some sentimental reason, she refused to sell it. She had no social security of her own, because she had never worked, only her and her husband's savings."

Lani had to start thinking about whether she wanted to accept the challenge of renovating the house and possibly moving here or not. She hadn't even had time to think about it and didn't now either, but it was definitely a money pit. She looked at the clock on her phone.

"Wow, I'm sorry, I have to go. I'm supposed to meet Alana for lunch."

"And I have to get to work," replied Max.

Lani had forgotten about that too.

"Oops! Sorry for keeping you so long! I thought this would be much faster."

"That's okay. I told my chief I wouldn't be there until noon."

He turned around and disappeared in the guesthouse. She just stood there for a second, watching him, dreamily.

Chapter 30

Alana was just locking up the gallery, when she saw Lani walking up from the parking lot. They smiled at each other and said "Hi", while they walked across the courtyard, into the restaurant of Hana Hotel, "The View". Of course Lani could see right away why the restaurant had earned that name, as she looked out of the window and saw the gorgeous gardens leading straight down to the ocean.

While they sat and waited for a menu, Alana stretched her arms across the table and took Lani's hands into hers. Her eyes were wet.

"You remind me so much of your mom. It's so nice to see you. It reminds me of the time when she and I were teenagers."

Lani waited and let Alana hold her hands. Lani felt an immediate bond with her.

"Your mom and I were really good friends. We told each other everything. Except when Paul showed up. She was so in love with him, she had no more time for me, but I didn't blame her, she was so happy."

"Did you meet him?"

"Not really, Luana would always go over to see him by herself. The rest of the gang stayed together. He'd paint these wonderful pictures of her and it was really kind of an intimate atmosphere, and we didn't want to bother them. But I did meet him later. He came back every year for a few years and kept trying to find Luana. He always rented the same cabin out by Waioka Pond and painted a lot. I was already working here, and he commissioned some of his paintings to the gallery and we sold them for him. Malani actually bought a lot of them when she could still afford it. Once there was an entire Paul Kent exhibition in the lobby. It was quite beautiful and successful. The lobby was packed almost every day."

"Do you know why he stopped coming?"

They got distracted. The waiter came and brought them the menus. Alana ate here so often that she didn't need one.

"Do you mind if I order for you?"

Lani was surprised, but since she basically ate everything, she didn't care.

"Sure!"

"Okay, we will both have the soup of the day and then some poi and after that the catch of the day, please. Mahalo."

"Sure, Alana," said the waiter and repeated the order.

Alana continued the conversation.

"No, I don't know why he suddenly stopped coming. Many of us were always looking forward to seeing him again and his new artwork, and one year he just didn't show up anymore. He left a void. Everyone in town liked having him around."

After a pause: "Luana left an even bigger void. Boy, do I miss her. Still today. She was such an upbeat positive person. Always kind and helpful. And we always had so much fun together. I will never forgive her father for treating her the way he did. It's his fault that she left and never came back. Luana's mother wasn't like him. She was too weak to fight him though. People in town feel sorry for her. He is a tyrant. I don't blame Malani for not speaking with him for 30 years."

Lani asked: "So, you said you took her to the ferry the day she left?"

"Yes. I will never forget that last day I saw her. She was quite desperate to get away from here. Sometimes I blame myself that she's gone, because I took her to the ferry."

She had tears in her eyes again and patted Lani's hand.

"One more thing comes to my mind," Alana added suddenly. "One day, Luana told me something about him possibly being married or having someone else. She had seen an article about him in a newspaper with a different woman. That made Luana quite upset. I can't imagine that it was true though. I seriously think she was the love of his life."

The soups came and they ate silently for a while. The food was delicious. Lani thought about what Alana had just told her. Had Luana just been an affair for Paul Kent? Another mystery she might never solve.

They finished lunch and Lani and Alana walked over to the gallery where Alana showed Lani some paintings that had a similar style to Paul Kent's. They were the works of Aaron, Pineapple Peter's younger brother, who had taken lessons from Paul Kent.

"You should talk to Aaron," said Alana. "Paul Kent gave him painting lessons for a while and they became friends. He lives in Paia and owns a gallery with his partner Mats." She looked around in a drawer and handed Lani a business card. "Here's his card. Very nice guys." Then she walked over to a corner in the back of the gallery. "Here are the Paul Kent prints that I wanted to show you. They're all limited editions, numbered and signed. Even these are quite valuable. One of the bigger originals, like the one at Koki Beach House, would go for around twenty thousand."

Lani gulped. She had no idea about prices for artwork, but it was a big surprise to her that her father's paintings were that valuable.

Chapter 31

After Lani had thanked Alana for lunch, said goodbye and left Hana Hotel, she thought it might be fun to stroll through the little "downtown" a bit and grab a few groceries at the Henderson Ranch Store. She was just about to cross the street, when she saw Max's pick-up drive by. She was going to lift her hand and wave, when she realized that there was another passenger in the truck: It looked like Mandy, who was laughing and holding her right arm out of the window, holding it in the wind... It felt like someone was stabbing a dagger through Lani's heart. She didn't really have any reason to be jealous. Was there even anything between her and Max? But didn't he feel the way about her that she felt about him? And why would he lie to her? He told her he had to work? Today he was hanging out with Mandy and tomorrow he was going to Lanai with her? I guess it's all just business with me, she thought.

What was supposed to be a relaxing day to get ready for Lanai had already turned into a busy day and now got even worse.
Walking up toward the Henderson Ranch Store, Lani suddenly discovered Leila, her grandmother. It looked like she was coming from the post office. Just as Leila was stepping off of the sidewalk into the street to get to the other side, a speeding truck drove up the road and Leila, startled, had to really jump back to not get hit. She stumbled and fell backwards over the edge of the sidewalk. She yelled out in pain and it looked like she couldn't get back up. Lani ran up to her.

"Are you okay?"

"No, I can't move my leg." Leila moaned. She looked like she was in a lot of pain. She realized that it was Lani and her eyes filled up with tears. She started babbling:

"I'm so sorry that I didn't help Luana. I was so weak and her father was such a tyrant. I should have put my foot down. But then she was suddenly gone one morning..." She started crying. "I'm so glad you're here now..."

"It's okay, it's okay. We can talk about that later. I think we have to call an ambulance."

She saw a tourist coming out of the post office and yelled:

"Help! Can you call an ambulance, please?!"

The tourist dialed 911. Minutes later, an ambulance with flashing lights drove up the road. Two paramedics jumped out and quickly checked out Leila. After a few minutes, they lifted her on a stretcher and into the ambulance.

"Are you a relative?" the older paramedic asked Lani. He thought she looked familiar.

"No. I just saw her fall." Lani replied.

"Thanks for calling us." replied the other paramedic who knew Leila. "We'll take her to the hospital and inform her husband."

"I'll be right over to check on her." Lani replied.

****

As Lani walked down the hallway, Kumu came walking toward her. He was just leaving. There was no way they could avoid each other. They both stopped.

"How is she?" Lani asked.

"She'll be okay. She broke her hip. She'll be in the hospital for a few days and then physical therapy. She told me you found and helped her. Mahalo."

Kumu continued.

"I was wrong. Pig-headed and stubborn. To let my actions be led by the fear of what the people in town think of me. Ho'oponopono. I'm sorry. I hope one day you can can forgive me for what I did to your mother."

Lani couldn't reply right now. She had a big lump in her throat. She just nodded and continued walking to Leila's room.

Kumu walked the other way.

There were three other older ladies in the room. It was more like at a party than in a hospital room. There were already flowers and balloons everywhere, the women were speaking Hawaiian and laughing loudly. When they saw Lani, they took her in their middle like an old friend.

"Luana's daughter! Come here. Give me a hug," said the first woman, walked up to Lani and embraced her cordially.
The second woman said: "You are just as beautiful as she was."
The third one said: "We're so glad to finally meet you."

Leila just smiled a broad smile, either because she was happy or because she was on so much pain medication. She could only reach Lani's hand from her bed and just patted it.

The ladies all chit-chatted happily and passed around Hawaiian candy, snacks, lilikoi and guava juice, and Lani felt like she had always been around them. She felt like she could forgive Leila. She wasn't so sure about Kumu, but he just seemed to be a sad old man. She might not ever be able to have a carefree relationship with him, but she felt more sorry for him than anything.
Finally, a nurse barged into the room and chased the ladies and Lani out.

"She just broke her hip, ladies! It's time to let her get some rest! Out!"

Chapter 32

Slowly, Lani drove back through Hana. Then she took a left onto Haneoo Road, passed Koki Beach and stopped at the Huli Huli chicken food truck, which she constantly stopped at to grab dinner and never got sick of. Malea, the girl who ran the food truck, and Lani greeted each other like old friends and chatted for a little while. Then Lani grabbed her plate of food and walked over to one of the benches close to the water. She just sat there and watched the ebb and flow of the tireless waves crashing onto the rocks. When they receded, it sounded like music.

Boy, she was going to miss this place when she went back home. She was going to have to make a decision soon…

She snapped out of her daydream when Max walked up, also with a plate of food.

He had seen her and stopped, since it was one of his favorite places as well, and it was much cheaper and easier to eat here than to buy groceries and cook.

"Hey, Lani, what's going on? How was the rest of your day?"

She was very reserved.

"Great."

"I heard at the fire station that Leila fell and broke her hip and that you were the one who found her!"

"Yup."

"That must have been quite awkward…"

She just nodded.

"How was lunch with Alana?"

"Great."

"The guys, Keanu and Billy, are great, you can be sure that they're going to give you really good prices and do the best they can. I'm very confident about them…"

"Uh huh."

Well, thought Max to himself, what's wrong with her? He stopped trying to have a conversation and ate silently, while he looked out at the ocean. Lani was done eating, so she gathered her silverware, plate and cup and got up.

"I'm not feeling well, I'm going to head back to the house, get ready for tomorrow and then call it an early night." she said.

"Okay, see you in the morning. We should leave fairly early. Is 8 am okay with you?"

"Sure. Good night."

She took her plate and utensils to a little dish cart next to the truck, said goodbye to Malea and headed home. She just wanted to be alone and not deal with Max and her thoughts about Mandy that kept gnawing at her. She didn't even know if she should go to Lanai with him....

When she arrived at Koki Beach House, the house and surroundings had a calming influence on her. She walked through the tropical backyard, enjoyed the plants, pulled some weeds and took some photos of blooming orchids and other flowers that she was going to text to her parents, Anne, Theresa and Sarah tomorrow. Looking at plants always made her happy and forget about all of her sorrows. Then she sat down on the swing by the ocean and watched the sun disappear behind the hills past Hamoa Beach and the sky turn all shades of yellow, red, pink and violet.

Chapter 33

The next morning, both Lani and Max were ready to depart at 8 am. They had decided to drive in Lani's little sedan, because it was more practical with a trunk to hide their luggage while traveling. Max was cautious this morning and tried not to be too talkative until he found out what had been bugging her last night.

Lani had decided that Max didn't owe her anything and that he could hang out with whomever he wanted. If he had a girlfriend he didn't want to tell her about, it was none of her business, since nothing had ever happened between them. So, she was upbeat and in her usual good mood and was in good spirits… or at least was pretending to be. She was looking forward to going to Lanai where her mother had probably stayed when she was pregnant with her. She also had the business card they had found in the cabin at Waioka Pond and she was planning on going to that gallery. It was nice to have some plans that might bring some new insight to the story.

They didn't stop until they reached Pineapple Peter's stand, because Lani wanted to talk to him again about her mother. Pineapple Peter looked up as Max and Lani parked, got out of the car and walked up. His face lit up when he recognized Max and he came around the counter to give him a big bear hug.

"Ke aloha ko'u hoa! Aloha, my friend! What's going on?"
Max replied and hugged him back. "Aloha".
Pineapple Peter looked at Lani, recognized her and greeted her too.

"Aloha." He continued and looked at Max. "So, you guys know each other?"

"Yup. Lani inherited Koki Beach House from Malani. She's her great niece."

"So, you really are Luana Kalekilio's daughter? I was pretty sure when I saw you the first time, but you didn't seem to know what I was talking about and it's really none of my business," said Peter.

"Well, it has been quite confusing," replied Lani. "I am trying to put bits and pieces of information like pieces of a puzzle together here and had never heard that last name. I seriously only came here because of the lawyer's letter I received about the house and I only knew Malani's name. Obviously Kahale was Malani's married name and Kalekilio her maiden name. And I can only guess that Luana was my mother. Everybody seems to recognize me, it's so strange, as if I'm a long lost friend…"

"Yes, I felt the same way when I first saw you. It's like your mom stepped back out of the past and never aged."

"You said you were good friends with her?"

"Yes, we knew each other since preschool and we're what you would call sandbox friends. Our parents were really good friends. I guess I was the one who they wanted as their son-in-law. We were just friends though, never in love. She told me a bit about Paul Kent and how much her father was against a relationship with a Haole. This whole thing also put a strain in my relationship between my parents and me. They were on Launa's parents side and of course I was on Luana's side…"

"But she never got in touch with you either after she had left?"

"Funny that you mention that. No, she didn't, but I was going to tell you something: She never got in touch with me, but a few years later, I was visiting my son Aaron who went to UH in Honolulu, and we both thought we saw her, just walking down Kalakaua Avenue, the main drag in Waikiki. As soon as I wanted to walk up to her and see if it was really her, she had disappeared. I looked her up in the white pages, but of course I didn't find her. She could have a different last name in the meantime. And of course I don't know if it was really her. Could have been a doppelganger."

Wow. Lani was excited. This was huge. Even though chances were slim, there was a tiny ray of hope that her mother was still alive.

"And when you're in Paia, you should definitely talk to Aaron. He and his partner Mats own a gallery there" continued Peter. "He might be able to give you some insight about Paul Kent. He hung out with him quite a bit…"

Lani replied "Yes, Alana already told me, you must also know Alana quite well, since she was Luana's best friend…"
Peter nodded. "We were all in the same class junior and senior year."

Max and Lani continued their drive to Lahaina after thanking Peter for the refreshments and the new input on Luana and Paul.

They were quiet most of the way, both in their thoughts and both enjoying the stunning views that the Hana Highway offered. It was a bright sunny day, mixed with a few showers and some rainbows and it was very humid on this side of the island that consisted of mostly rain forest. Soon they arrived in Paia.

"Shall we go and see Aaron in his gallery? I'd love to talk to him." Lani asked.

"Yes, definitely, but what do you think about getting some lunch first?" replied Max. "I'm starving. My buddy Lenny is one of the managers at Paia Mahi House. It's right on the main drag. They have the best Mahi sandwiches ever."

Chapter 34

They parked the car and walked up the main road. Paia Mahi House was buzzing. It was noon, the busiest time of the day, the place was packed, all tables and benches seemed to be taken, but, to Lani's surprise, Max just walked past the line at the counter, stepped into the kitchen and shouted:

"Hey, Lenny. One table for a VIP, please!"

Lenny, a very big Hawaiian man about the same age as Max and Lani came up, started beaming all over his face when he saw Max and they both gave each other a big bear hug.

"Hey, buddy, how are you doing? Long time no see!" said Lenny with a very loud deep voice with the same Hawaiian accent that Max had. Then he spotted Lani, who had followed Max hesitantly, released Max out of his strong grip and asked:

"Well, who is this beautiful young lady?"

Lani blushed.

"It's my friend Lani. We're on our way to Lanai."

Lenny greeted Lani with a smile and shook her hand.

"Hey, nice to meet you Lani!" he said, looking from Lani to Max. "Guys, make sure you check out the Lanai Bed & Breakfast. It's been there forever and has turned out to be a really nice little place."

"Thanks, Lenny. We're definitely going to check it out. We're starving. Is there anything you can do about a table?" asked Max.

Lenny walked to the front and called a young waitress who was just grabbing some plates from the counter to take them into the dining-room.

"Becky, can you please give the next available table to Max? He's in a bit of a hurry."

"Sure, boss!" she replied and nodded at Max and Lani. "One of our best tables in the front actually just became available. Follow me, folks."

"Thanks, Lenny," said Max and gave him a fist bump, while he and Lani followed Becky to the front of the restaurant.

The mahi sandwiches with a side of fries and cole slaw and some fresh guava juice were delicious. They just sat and enjoyed their lunch and watched the crowd for a while, until Max looked at the clock on his phone and was a bit shocked about how late it was already.

"Oh, wow, it's already past four. I guess we'd better go and check how late Aaron's gallery is open if we want to see him today."

"I agree," replied Lani.

Max made "Check please!" motions to Becky, who came right up and said:

"Lenny is in a meeting and said to say bye to you. Lunch is on the house," said Becky with a smile.

"Thank you!" they both said simultaneously and Max left a generous tip for Becky.

They walked down the main road and then turned into a side street and came up to the gallery that they were looking for and that Aaron, Pineapple Peter's brother and his partner owned: "HO'ONANI", which was the verb that described beauty. The gallery was certainly beautiful. The colorful artwork was outstanding and they could already tell that lots of the paintings were from Aaron himself and even a few pieces from Paul Kent.

A very tall handsome Scandinavian looking young man was talking to a customer.

"Excuse me for a second," he said to his customer, while he turned around and greeted Max and Lani.

"Aloha, are you Mats?" asked Max. "We're friends of Peter's and are looking for Aaron.

"Aloha... I'm sorry, guys. He's actually in Honolulu for some meetings today. He won't be back until late tomorrow. Do you want to come back?"

"Yes, we're actually heading back to Hana the day after tomorrow, so it might work out on Sunday, if you guys are available then. He might remember me, I'm Max. Max Palakiko."

"Okay, I'll let him know you were here."

"Can I take a card? Then I can call when we leave Lahaina on Sunday and check if he's available."

"Sure thing. Good idea."

"You have some beautiful artwork," said Lani. "Do you mind if we look around a bit? I'm especially interested in the Kent paintings. It looks like you have a few."

"Yes, they are actually from Aaron's private collection and not for sale. He was friends with Paul."

"Sorry for the interruption," Lani said to the other customer.

"No worries, I'm a friend of Mats' and just stopped by," answered the other customer with a smile.

"Well, mahalo and we hope to see you on Sunday," said Max.

Chapter 35

It was time to continue their trip to Lahaina. They got into the car and drove the pretty route past Iao Valley and along the West Maui Mountains on the right and beaches on the left in the beautiful afternoon light.

They drove into the historical town of Lahaina that had been transformed into a Maui hotspot with a variety of unique shops, art galleries and restaurants. It was a very busy time in the late afternoon when people had returned from their day trips and were ready for dinner and some shopping. Tourists were milling about everywhere, so Max slowed down and they enjoyed the busy atmosphere, driving into town with their windows down. They passed the big famous banyan tree and Max took a right into a side street, where he turned into a long driveway that took them into a private parking lot behind the row of buildings.

While they got out of the car, Max said:

"Why don't you leave your duffle bag in the car for now. My friends Julia and Tony are probably both at the restaurant. He manages the place and she's the chef. We can walk over there to say hello and then walk around and go shopping or just have some drinks until we're hungry and go back for dinner. Their apartment is right up here."

He pointed up at the building in front of the parking lot. She nodded and followed him back to Front Street. They walked around, had some shave ice, just enjoyed being carefree and among all the lucky vacationers in one of the most beautiful spots in the world.

Then they sat down on a small beach on the side of the harbor and watched the sunset. It was a bit too romantic for Lani, because thoughts of Mandy were still in her head. She jumped up, a bit antsy.

"Would you mind if I went shopping for a little while? I have to buy some gifts for my friends and family at home. This seems to be the perfect place, and I'm not even sure if I'll ever have a chance again. There's not much shopping in Hana besides the expensive gallery…"

"Sure." He was a bit disappointed, because he enjoyed hanging out with her. He looked at his watch. "It's 6:30 now. Shall we say 8 pm at Tony's? I'm not that hungry anyhow after that giant lunch…"

"Same. See you at 8." She smiled at him, turned around and walked back up toward Front Street, where she disappeared in between the droves of people.

Max just sat there, staring at her back, thinking: Why are things always so complicated?

****

It was already 8:15 pm. Lani walked up to the restaurant, breathless and with giant steps, with several shopping bags in her hands. She had totally lost track of time and hated making people wait. Max was sitting at a nice window table by himself, looking at his watch, when she walked up.

"I'm so sorry, I totally lost track of time!"

"That's okay, I've been hanging out and chatting with Julia and Tony. It's fine. They are a bit busy right now, but I'll introduce you as soon as I get a chance. It looks like you scored in the shops?"

She smiled. "Yes, I found some awesome gifts for my mom and best friends Theresa and Sarah and my assistant Anne. The guys are harder. I have to get something for my dad and this guy who's taking care of my nursery."

"Get them a bone fish hook." He got his hook on a leather band out of his shirt and showed her. "All guys like these."

In this instance, Max's friend Julia walked up with a big Italian appetizer platter with sautéed peppers and zucchini, olives, Caprese salad, rolled up prosciutto and some vittelo tonnato.

"Aloha, you must be Lani," she said to Lani and shook her hand. "It's nice to finally meet you. Here, I made this just for you guys. Antipasto misto, one of our specialties."

"Nice to meet you too! Wow, that looks amazing. I don't think I'll need a main course anymore after this." said Lani.

"Yes, it looks delicious," added Max. "Thanks, Julia!"

"Enjoy. Sorry, I have to get back to work. I'll see you guys later. I'll have Bianca bring you guys some garlic bread and house wine." said Julia.

They ate as much as they could, but they both weren't very hungry after the late lunch.

Finally, the kitchen closed and the restaurant was empty and Julia and Tony joined them.

"Thanks for a great dinner." said Lani.

"Our pleasure." replied Tony. "Friends of Max, friends of ours."

"So, what brings you here?" asked Julia. "Or are you just on vacation?"

Lani and Max told them the whole story or what they knew of it. Lani's mother was seen in Lanai the last time right after Lani was born and they also told them what they knew about her father, who had obviously been a renowned artist and had somehow mysteriously been deleted from the internet. Julia and Tony looked at each other with big eyes.

"I don't want to tell you horror stories," started Julia, "but years ago a tragic story about a famous artist made the rounds, who was in love with a Hawaiian girl. She disappeared from the face of the Earth and he was never able to find her. Because of that, he was obsessed with painting her again and again. Did you never hear this story, Max? One winter, he was on his way to his retreat in Hana where he stayed and painted every year. This time he had been warned to stay off the road, because the weather was so stormy and rainy and there was a really bad risk of mudslides. But he was so eager to get there and went anyhow… He was supposedly hit by a landslide in a sharp hair-pin needle curve and pushed down the side of the cliff in his car and died. His car was salvaged, but he was never found. The name of the artist was Paul something."

Lani's eyes filled with tears. She tried to remain calm, but she couldn't. She jumped up, excused herself and walked out of the restaurant. She was embarrassed about her own outburst, but she was sure that this story was about her own father. Max excused himself too, followed her and tried to console her, but she was very emotional.

"Don't you agree that it might be my father?"

"Yeah, unfortunately it sounds like it..."

"This whole trip is a nightmare, I'm just uncovering tragedy after tragedy. Shall I even continue?"

She walked over to a low wall by the ocean that some couples were sitting on, happily chatting in the moonlight, and stared out at the water.

Max followed her, took her in his arms and just held her while she cried. Then she looked up. It felt so good to have his arms wrapped around her. She stared into his dark eyes, and their lips finally met for what seemed an endless kiss...

Chapter 36
Lanai

The next morning, as the sun was just about to go up, Max and Lani ran up to the dock where the older ticket saleslady of the Ferry to Lanai was just closing her booth. Max ran up to the booth and pleaded for her to reopen the booth and sell them two more tickets. And, of course she was also an old friend of his and she reopened the booth with a smile.

"For you always, Max! What are you doing on Lanai?"

"My friend Lani has to go and I'm just coming along," he said with a smile.

"I wish you'd join me one day…" she flirted with him and they both laughed, while Lani looked at him from the side. Did everyone flirt with Max, and this early in the morning? Seriously? She rolled her eyes. She needed coffee.

Max looked at Lani and grinned.

"Thanks, my love!" he said to the ticket saleslady. "We'll take two round trips. We're coming back tonight."

The ferry ride in the sunrise was just delightful. The ocean was so calm that it almost looked like a mirror, both the sky and the ocean looked like an artist's canvas, dipped in all shades of red, pink and purple. As the sun slowly rose, the colors turned into a beautiful blue, the sky just a touch lighter than the dark blue ocean.

It was still whale season, so everyone on board kept a sharp eye out for them. And soon someone in the bow called out…: "Whale!" A whale and her calf were both breaching. We could see the exuberant display of the majestic whales jumping up and going back under the surface for quite a while. While everyone was waiting for the whales to resurface, the Captain explained:

"Whales can hold their breath for up to twenty minutes."

As the mother and her calf came back up, Lani rushed over to the bow of the boat and watched the incredible creatures, speechless. Max followed her. Even though the whales were so amazing, he only had eyes for Lani. He looked at her beautiful skin that was shining in the sunlight and the way she was concentrating on the gentle giants. They hadn't exchanged any signs of infatuation since last night, but he craved being close to her and carefully placed his arm around her shoulder. Surprised, she looked up, she loved feeling the warmth of his muscular body, returned his embrace and gently kissed him on the lips. They just stood there, their eyes gazing at each other, while they were too distracted to watch the end of the whales' magnificent display…

Lani and Max sat on the outside deck of the ferry, just watching the beauty that surrounded them. The cool breeze and the salty air felt wonderful on Lani's skin. She just enjoyed the spiritual magic of Hawaii that embraced all of its visitors. The ferry chugged along, and slowly, Lanai's red rugged coastline became more visible. Lanai looked wild and uncultivated, a bit deserted. Lani couldn't imagine that people lived there. She spotted a pod of Hawaiian spinner dolphins, jumping in and out of the water and pointed. Max looked and smiled.

The ferry drove into a smaller harbor and anchored at a dock while the Captain told the passengers a few things about Lanai.
"Ladies and Gentlemen, welcome to Lanai. Lanai is the sixth largest of the Hawaiian Islands. It is known as the pineapple island because of its past as an island-wide pineapple plantation. The islands only settlement is the small town of Lanai City. Many of the island's landmarks are accessible only by dirt roads that require a four-wheel drive vehicle. There is one school Lanai High and Elementary School, serving the entire island from Kindergarten through 12th grade. There is also one hospital, Lanai Community Hospital, with 24 beds…"
Lani listened up when she heard Lanai Community Hospital and said to Max:
"We should go and check out the hospital too. I was probably born there. Maybe they still have those records."
Max nodded. "Good idea."

"And," Lani pulled out the business card from the gallery she had found in Paul Kent's little cabin, "we should check out this gallery too."

The passengers disembarked the ferry, while the Captain announced the time that the ferry was returning to Maui. "Ladies and Gentlemen, the last ferry to Lahaina departs at 6 pm. If you wish to return with us, please don't be late. We wish you a nice stay in Lanai."

Max had rented a Jeep, so they had to go to the car rental booth first, but soon they were on their way to Lanai City.

Chapter 37

Lani and Max started their search for any information about Luana by stopping at some stores and restaurants, but people were not very talkative and most newer shop owners were too young to even know what had happened 30 years ago… They walked up to a rinky-dink gift shop and art gallery, which actually happened to be the same one on Lani's business card. Two ladies in their late fifties were sitting inside, laughing heartily about a guy in his late thirties, who they were obviously harassing in a good-natured manner. He slinked out of the gallery as the ladies laughed and shouted: "See you later, handsome…!"

"Haha, hey guys, boy, that guy did not have a very good sense of humor!" The owner, sitting behind the counter, laughed with her friend in front of the counter, as she slapped her knee and drank another sip of wine. A half empty bottle was standing on the counter, next to two glasses.

"What happened?" asked Max, grinning.

"Oh, we were just hitting on him and actually invited him to a party tonight, but he didn't seem very interested when I told him we needed him to jump out of the cake with just his birthday suit on!" she giggled. They all laughed about that idea.

"Just some good-natured fun. People have no sense of humor anymore nowadays! Now he's going to join the "Me Too" movement…" she said and laughed. "By the way, I'm Lisa Holmquist, and this is my friend Jill. Can I help you guys find anything?"
Max introduced Lani and himself to the ladies. "Hi, I'm Max and this is my friend Lani."
Lani said: "Hi, ladies". She got the old yellowed business card out and put it on the counter. "It looks like this is your card," she said to Lisa. "We found this in a cabin where the painter Paul Kent used to stay."
Lisa picked up the old business card and looked at it from both sides.

"Yes, that is my card. Quite an old one," she confirmed.

Lani and Max told the ladies about Paul Kent, who painted a girl many times who looked just like Lani and about the painting in Koki Beach House.

"We think he might be my father," added Lani.

The two women looked at each other, then at Lani.

"Yes, you do look exactly like the girl in the painting," said Lisa. She led them to a painting in the back of the gallery.

This is one of them," she continued. "The other big one, with the girl in it who looks exactly like you, was sold to the owners of Lanai Bed & Breakfast. It's just about five minutes away. Paul Kent was a friend of mine. He used to come here and sell paintings to me until he died in the terrible car crash. Real nice guy. Very quiet and soft-spoken. He always seemed a bit melancholic…"

Lani and Max looked each other with big eyes, when Lisa mentioned the car crash again.

"Do you know anything about the car crash?" asked Lani. "There's nothing about it online."

"No, I just know that he was warned not to drive, but I guess he was extremely anxious to get to Hana… and that he was never found. Only the car. But that's no surprise with that thick jungle over there…"

"Did he ever speak to you about Luana, my mother?"

"No. He was very quiet and didn't speak much at all. Very private. I was curious who the girl in the paintings was, but never asked him. The name Luana does ring a bell though. I think that might be the name of the other painting."

"Take care of that handsome guy of yours." said Lisa's friend Jill to Lani with a grin in her face, nudging Lisa in the ribs, as Max and Lani were getting ready to leave.

Lisa and Jill both giggled, while Lani and Max shook their hands.

"Mahalo, ladies. It was nice to meet you both," said Max, trying to ignore the fact that they were both quite tipsy and now starting to hit on him…

"Come back anytime," Jill said flirtatiously, "especially you, Max!" And they both started giggling again.

Chapter 38

Lani and Max walked over to Lanai Bed & Breakfast, which was a small hotel with a really nice restaurant.

"This has to be the bed & breakfast where Luana stayed and worked 30 years ago." said Max. "It's basically the only bed & breakfast on the island besides a couple of big resorts."

They walked up to the restored former plantation home, which was built in 1925 for pineapple executives. It was a beautiful old building with shutters on the windows and a wraparound porch. They entered and walked into the lobby where they immediately discovered the painting of Luana the two women in the gallery had talked about. It was gorgeous and matched the one in Koki Beach House. Lani walked up to it and looked for the signature "Paul Kent" at the bottom right. It looked like it had been painted later than the other one, in 1991.

They walked up to the front desk and introduced themselves to the younger owner or manager of the hotel. He had a nametag on his shirt, which said Jacob Smith.

"Aloha," said Lani. "I'm Lani Winters and this is Max Palakiko. What a beautiful hotel!"

"Aloha and Mahalo. We do our best to keep it in good shape. It's actually a historical landmark," Jacob replied proudly.

"We are looking for someone who might know if my mother worked here about thirty years ago. Her name was or is Luana Kalekilio. My mother must have been pregnant back then. You're obviously too young to remember," Lani added with a smile.

"No, not really," he answered laughing. He was in his early to mid thirties. "I actually do remember her. She was our nanny when I was about four or five years old. My mother never stopped working in the hotel, even when she had us kids. Luana was awesome. But she had her baby four weeks early and then suddenly disappeared. It's a bit of a tragic story... Maybe my mom knows more. She's on the back patio."

Jacob stepped away from the front desk and led them to his mother, an elegant woman in her 70s, Elizabeth Smith. She was sitting in a rocking chair on the back patio, teaching a parrot in a cage how to say something. She was surrounded by beautiful orchids and other tropical flowers.

"My mother doesn't see and hear very well anymore." Jacob explained. He spoke in a very loud clear voice:

"Mom, I brought some people who would like to ask you some questions. This is Lani and this is Max. Lani is looking for her mother Luana, remember her? She was our nanny when I was about four or five."

Elizabeth stopped taking to the parrot and looked up at the visitors. Since the sun was right behind Lani, she couln't see her. She grabbed a cane that was leaning against her chair, got up slowly and walked a bit closer up to Lani. She stared up into Lani's face, which was a bit awkward, but they could tell that she had a hard time seeing. As she recognized how much Lani looked like Luana, Elizabeth's eyes filled with tears.

"My dear child, you certainly look like your mother. She was such a hardworking wonderful girl. The kids loved her."

She continued: "Even though she had such a hard time. The work was not easy for someone who was pregnant… she ended up having the baby four weeks early, maybe because it was too much for her… Jacob is the oldest, so she had to take care of three little children under five when I was working... her water suddenly broke one day…"
Lani and Max just let her talk.

"I am so glad to see you doing so well, my child. It was such a sad day when Luana left and you were in the hospital, all alone. She just walked out of the hospital and disappeared… She was seen near the cliffs by Puu Pehe, and people think she jumped, but I don't think she was the type to do something like that. Too much zest for life..."

"Why do you think noone in the family took me? Like Malani, for example?" asked Lani.

"Malani had promised Luana to take you to the orphanage. She wanted you far away from Hana. The authorities would have probably taken you away from Malani and given you to the maternal grandparents. She didn't want them to have you after what they put her through. Malani was very unhappy to have to give you away, but even though the adoption process was strictly confidential, she found out somehow where you were and knew you were having a happy childhood. Do you know that she sent money for you?"

"Yes, my parents just recently told me. They saved it and gave it to me for this trip. Otherwise I wouldn't have been able to afford it," she said, looking at Max.

Elizabeth continued: "We all had promised Luana that we wouldn't say anything, but the police never showed up here. It looks like everyone helping Luana and Malani stuck together and never told anyone that she came to Lanai. Malani told me that Luana's parents never found out whether she had a baby or not." She thought for a second. "Have they seen you yet? It must have been quite a shock for them…"

Lani nodded.

Elizabeth took Lani's hand and pulled her inside to the lobby. She stopped in front of the painting.

"I saw this in the gallery one day and had to buy it, even though I spent half of the kids' college funds. I really wanted it as a memory, because it's definitely Luana. I never met the artist Paul Kent, but I assume he is your father…"

Lani nodded. "I think he's my father too. Unfortunately, it looks like he's dead."

"Ohhh, I'm so sorry to hear that," replied Elizabeth and caressed Lani's cheek.

Elizabeth turned around abruptly toward her son behind the front desk.

"Jacob, I want her to have the painting. It's hers now."

Jabob's, Lani's and Max's jaws dropped. The painting was very valuable. Lani caught herself quickly.

"No, Ms. Elizabeth. It's yours. For helping Luana when she needed it most."

They gave each other a hug, both of them had tears in their eyes.

Chapter 39

Lani's and Max's next stop was the Lanai Community Hospital. Lani felt quite sentimental to see the building where she probably was born and where her desperate young mother had left her. They stepped inside and walked over to the reception desk.

"Aloha… um… we wanted to look at some medical records, if possible…" started Lani.

The busy receptionist cut her off. "If you want medical records, you'd have to call or go and see the medical records department. We usually only keep medical records for six years, but if they're yours and you were an infant at that time, we might still have them. The medical records department is down this hallway and then down the first stairway on your left, right past the elevators."

She was so busy that she turned away and answered the phone without even waiting for a reply. They started walking down the hallway the receptionist had pointed at, but, as they passed an elevator, Lani discovered a sign that said "Maternity Ward". She pressed the elevator button, pulled Max inside and the door closed.

"We can look for medical records later. I just want to go and take a look at the Maternity Ward."

Max was shocked about Lani's sudden spontaneity. They certainly wouldn't be allowed to enter the maternity ward, but Lani didn't seem to care. The elevator arrived on the third floor with a "ding" and they stepped out. The hallway was empty. They walked in as if they were regular visitors. Lani looked around and found the nursery with a few babies in it. They looked inside through the big window.

"May I help you! Are you here to visit someone?" asked an older nurse with a stern voice.

"Ummm… no, we're actually lost…" stammered Lani. She couldn't think of a better excuse.

Max was really embarrassed and said to Lani, almost whispering: "Let's get out of here…"

"You need to leave right away, or I'll call security. You have no business here."

She walked up to Lani and Max and looked into their faces. She hesitated when she looked up in Lani's face.

"Hang on a second... You remind me of someone. A patient we had here a long time ago, who was very special and dear to me. I had just started working here, was in my early twenties, and she was even younger, maybe 17 or 18..."

"Yes, that was most likely my mother. I'm looking for information about her. I was adopted and never met her, but I recently inherited a house in Hana from my great-aunt. I am finding out a lot about my mother, but mostly that she disappeared after having me and was never seen again. We're trying to figure out what might have happened to her. Would you mind answering a few questions about her?"

"Let's go and sit down. Would you both like a coffee?"

They sat down in the nurse's lounge, and the nurse, who introduced herself as Christel, brought some coffee and cookies.

They chatted a little, but then Lani couldn't wait any longer and asked the most pressing question. "Do you think my mother could have jumped off of the cliffs of Puu Pehe?"

"To answer your question, I don't know if she jumped off of the cliffs. I only saw her when she was already in labor, and after having a baby your hormones go crazy. That's why so many young moms get post-partum depression. She seemed depressed, just cried and cried, asking for someone named Paul. That's why I sat with her as much as I could. I had just ended a 14 hour shift and gone home when she somehow left here without being seen by anyone, not even security. Big failure of the hospital. There were no security cameras back then like we have now. I wish I could have held her back. But after she left, I spoke with the owners of the Lanai Bed & Breakfast, and they said she had been serious at times, but usually an upbeat happy girl."

Again, no new information. One person said one thing, the next person said the opposite. They spoke for a little while longer and Max and Lani got up, thanked Nurse Christel and left. It seemed the mystery around Luana would never get solved.

They went down to the medical records department, but the attendant wouldn't even let them know whether there were medical records for Luana Kalekilio.

"Sorry," said the clerk. "I can't give you this information. It falls under doctor-patient confidentiality. You'd have to request the information in writing and add your birth certificate to prove that you're Ms. Kalekilio's child."

Chapter 40

Their last stop was almost just for sentimental reasons. They knew that they wouldn't find any signs of Luana at the cliffs by Puu Pehe after such a long time, but Lani had to go there and see what her mom had seen thirty years ago. It helped her that Elizabeth had said that she didn't think Luana killed herself, although Christel's words made her uneasy again.

Then Max read the story of Puu Pehe to her in a brochure of Lanai.

"According to Legend, a young Hawaiian warrior from Lanai captured a beautiful princess from the island of Maui, who he was going to marry. Afraid that other men would see how beautiful she was, the warrior hid the princess in a sea cave near Puu Pehe. One day, a Kona storm made the weather change so drastically, that the water level rose and the beautiful princess drowned in the sea cave. Heartbroken, the warrior carried the princess to the top of Puu Pehe where he buried her. Stricken with grief, he jumped to his death from the top of Puu Pehe."

"Wow, what a fitting spot this tragic place is for my mother's own tragic story. I hope she didn't behave like the warrior or, even worse, hide in the sea cave and drown..." she shuddered thinking about that possibility.

"Don't worry. You can't even get to those caves without a boat," replied Max. "She had no chance of getting down there. So, that didn't happen..."

Lani felt relieved.

They just stood there, on the red cliffs, overlooking the smooth blue ocean, the big rock knows as "Pehe's Tomb" and Shark's Cove which you could only access by boat. The wind was blowing in their faces. They tried to go back in time in their thoughts, wondering what Luana thought when she stood here thirty years ago, not knowing where to go and having just left her child. How strange that this area, where Luana had supposedly been seen last, had been the scene of such a tragic legend.

Max and Lani took one last glance at the glistening blue and green ocean before heading back. The sun was already standing quite low and it was almost golden hour. Max looked at the clock on his phone. He was shocked. It was 5:30 and the last ferry left at 6 pm!

"Oh, no!" said Max. "It's 5:30. I totally lost track of time. We have to really hurry up if we want to get back to the harbor, return the Jeep and catch the ferry at 6!"

"Let's go!" replied Lani.

They rushed over to the Jeep, got in and Max accelerated with squealing tires, stirring up a cloud of dust.

The ferry had already departed when they arrived at the harbor.

"Oh, well, I guess it really doesn't make a difference?" said Max. "We would have had to stay overnight in Lahaina anyway. This way, we just take the first ferry in the morning and go straight back to Hana."

"That's right. Just too bad, I would have loved to see more of the West side of the island tomorrow, but maybe I won't be here the last time," replied Lani. "I guess we'll have to go back to Lanai Bed & Breakfast and get some rooms."

They drove back to Lanai Bed & Breakfast, but there was only one room available. Lani slept on the bed and Max on the pull-couch, but it wasn't very comfortable. They both tossed and turned. They were both too tense about being in one bedroom ... finally, Lani got up and pulled Max into her bed, where they shyly started kissing, but then became more and more passionate and made love for the first time…

The next morning, Lani finally had to know what was going on with the singer Mandy who still spooked through her head. During breakfast in the beautiful breakfast room of Hotel Lanai she finally broached the subject.

"Max, ummm… can I ask you a question?"

He hesitated. What did this have to mean? But then he said "Sure, what's going on?"

"The day after we saw your friend Mandy at Hana Hotel, I saw you and her driving through town, looking quite comfortable together. Are you sure there was never anything going on between the two of you?"

"Oh, God, that! Yes, I'm sure. She is such a drama queen. She had a flat tire and called the fire department because she needed help. Seriously, to call the fire department... I had just arrived, so they turned me around and sent me to pick her up and have her tire fixed. Trust me, there's really nothing going on between her and me. I hope she's gone by the time we're back."

"Hmmm. Okay. I guess it's not your fault you're so hot", Lani replied and grinned at him.
They both had to laugh.

"Thanks for the compliment." Max looked deep into her eyes and took both of her hands into his while he leaned forward to give her a kiss across the table.

The ferry ride back to Lahaina was beautiful, this time they sat very close to each other, but didn't have eyes for the magnificent surroundings, just for each other. Max called Aaron's gallery to check if they could see them on their way back through Paia. He was available in the late morning, which gave them just enough time to get there.

Chapter 41

They arrived in Paia and found a parking space right in front of the *"HO'ONANI"* gallery, which was very lucky, since it was always busier on a Sunday morning than in the week. Both Mats and Aaron were there, taking care of a well-dressed customer who was wearing very expensive designer clothes. Max and Lani nodded at them, but let them do their sales spiel and looked around in the gallery without interrupting them. Mats and Aaron quietly nodded at them. The customer finally bought a contemporary painting for about $10,000.— and it took another 15 minutes to discuss the details about shipping the painting to her home in California. They remained as cool as cucumbers until she had walked out and disappeared around the corner, but then they jumped up and down like little boys, hugged and high fived each other, including Max and Lani.

"Yay! That made our day! Or let's say week!" said Aaron.

"Or let's say month!" added Mats and they hugged each other happily.

Aaron turned toward Lani and Max. "Don't get me wrong, people spend a lot of money on art here in Paia, but that's still a special sale and that painting has been here for a while. I'm glad we finally get to switch it out."

He stretched his hand out to shake Lani and Max's. "You must be Lani and Max. Mats and Peter told me about you. It's very nice to meet you. Did you already look around the first time you were here?"

"Yes, your artwork is stunning. It really does look a bit similar to my father's." replied Lani.

Aaron smiled. "I take that as a compliment. He was an unbelievable painter." he paused for a second. "I'd like to take you to our house. You're not going to believe it when you see it, but we have an awesome painting of Paul's in our living-room. Really beautiful. You have to see it. Our house is right down the road. After that," he turned around and looked at Mats. "Can you close the gallery for an hour or so? I'd like to celebrate the sale with these guys at Mama's and we can chat a little about Paul." He looked at Lani and Max while he explained with a smile and put his arm around Mats's shoulder. "Mats knew him quite well too - we've been together for fifteen years."

Lani and Max nodded and smiled.

"Congrats on the sale. Are you sure you want to go to Mama's? It's quite the pricey place", said Max.

"Yeah, don't worry about it. You're my guest. I know the owner, so she gives me a special rate and always has a nice table for us. I provide artwork for the interior and helped them redesign the place recently, and I take clients there. We help each other out a lot."

"You'll love it!", said Max, looking at Lani. "It's the best restaurant in Maui."

"I agree", replied Aaron. He looked at Mats. "Can you meet us there in about an hour?"

Mats nodded. "Sure. Text me when you leave the house and head over there."

Lani was excited. She had read a lot of excellent reviews about Mama's Fish House.

Aaron proposed: "Why don't I ride with you guys, and then I can drive with Mats on the way back."

"Great idea," replied Max. "Just tell me where to go." Max took a right out of the parking space and had to do a u-turn first.

"Now go down to the T in the road and take a right onto Hana Highway," Aaron directed him.

Max took a right and they were heading out of town. They came up to a nice area with oceanfront villas on the left and after just about half a mile, Aaron told him to take a left into a driveway. All they could see from the street was a big wall, but as they drove into the gravel driveway and Aaron opened the gate with a pin number, a small beautiful oasis right on the ocean unfolded before them. It was a very contemporary white square shaped three story-house surrounded by tall palm trees. From the front door, they could see the ocean straight through the house. They walked inside the house, and Lani knew immediately what Aaron had meant with special painting. A tryptich, a

three-paneled painting, covered the one and only wall that wasn't glass
or leading into the open kitchen with stainless steel appliances and white
stone countertops. The painting covered a big part of the wall and
looked almost like a mural and like the beach and a tropical rainforest
continued into the house. It was amazing. They just stood there silently,
looking at the details and taking in its beauty.
Aaron asked: "Did I promise too much? Your father was a genius."

"It's just amazing. Your whole house is amazing." replied Lani and
looked around. "You live in paradise."

"Seriously. I am very thankful to your father. He gave me a lot of
good advice. Not only regarding painting. Also about marketing my own
paintings and about opening up the gallery. He was a great and selfless
guy. He led a quite simple life and didn't care much for luxury. The only
money he needed, I guess, was to keep traveling here and keep his nice
house on the river in the Thousand Islands. Oh, there was one thing. He
loved antique boats. Mats and I actually visited him in Clayton once. It's
beautiful up there," he grinned and added: "but I've only been there in
the summer. Too cold in the winter!"
He reflected for a second. "If he actually really died, I wonder what
happened to his house and his boats up there. His parents were really
old, and he never got married or had other kids."

That opened up a whole new series of questions for Lani. But the
Thousand Islands were really not that far from the Hudson Valley,
maybe a five or six hour drive. She was definitely going to drive up and
check if she could find any traces of her father there and look for the
gallery and talk to people at the college he had worked at.

"I see your head is spinning with all this information," said Aaron
and looked at his watch. "I think we have to go now. I told Mats we'd be
at Mama's at 12:30. It's 12:15 now. We should go."

Chapter 42
Mama's Fish House

They got back into the car, Aaron texted Mats that they were on their way, and they drove another few miles down the winding road along the coast and arrived at Mama's Fish House. People were dressed up and we could tell that they came here for special occasions. Lani felt quite underdressed in her blouse, shorts and flip flops in what felt to her like a Hollywood movie setting, but she was wrong. She looked wonderful. She had inherited the same natural beauty from her mother, but just wasn't aware of it, since she was more a nature-loving tomboy.

Mats wasn't there yet, but the hostess seated them anyhow. Everyone, hostess, waiters and barkeepers, greeted Aaron like a long-lost friend. As soon as Mats had arrived and was sitting in the fourth chair, the Maitre d', Antonio, a young, Italian, very good-looking guy, came up with quick steps and kissed Aaron and Mats on both cheeks.

"Aloha, i miei amici!" he said in a mixture of Hawaiian and Italian. "It's so good to see you! I'm sorry, but Mama isn't here right now. I'm not sure if you'll see her today, but I'll let her know you're here and maybe she can return sooner."

"Oh, please don't tell her to interrupt her day. We need to get back to the gallery anyhow and these guys still have to drive all the way to Hana. These are my friends, Lani and Max from Hana. Lani and Max, this is Antonio. He's the Maitre d' here. Really great guy! Be nice to him and you'll get the best treatment in this wonderful gourmet temple."

"Oh, mio Dio, you're making me blush, my friend! Shall I bring you a combination of the usual appetizers?"

"Yes, please just bring us something to share. Do you guys like sushi?" he asked Lani and Max, who nodded. "And please bring us a bottle of champagne too! We're celebrating a really big sale today," Aaron explained to Antonio and then he looked at Max and Lani again. "I know you guys can't drink a lot because of the drive you have ahead of you, but you can at least toast with us!"

Max and Lani nodded and smiled.

"Do you guys mind if I just let Antonio bring us the restaurant's catch of the day and some other specialties? That's what I usually do and I've never gone wrong with that."

"Sounds good." replied Lani and Max nodded again.

"Antonio, we'll have four catches of the day, please."

"Perfect choice. Coming right up!" replied Antonio.

While waiters were bringing poi, a Hawaiian specialty made of mashed taro plant, and bread, as well a little sample of fish soup for everyone and water for the table, Lani looked at Aaron. She was anxious to find out more about Paul Kent.

"Aaron, can you tell us more about Paul Kent? You're not older than in your mid to late thirties, so you must have met him much later than the summer he met my mother, right?"

"Haha, thanks for the compliment, I'm actually 42. But you're right. I didn't meet him until I was in my junior year in High School when I started becoming really serious about painting. Let me think… I was 17, so I met him 25 years ago. And you are how old?

"29, so he and my mother met 30 years ago."

"Okay, so this was five years after he met your mother. I had skipped school like unfortunately I did too often… I was out painting somewhere, I think it was at Hamoa Beach, and he came up to paint as well. Just by coincidence, I had chosen his favorite spot. We just started painting together and talked and he gave me a lot of advice. He eventually took me to his cabin to give me some lessons, where I saw the paintings of your mom for the first time. They were everywhere and one more beautiful than the other. He said she was the love of his life. He never got over her. Always seemed so melancholic. In the middle of a conversation, he'd just space out and stare at the ocean for ages. I'd get really antsy, but I didn't want to bother him, so I'd just be quiet and go about my business or continue painting, although it did make me nervous. I mean, because I worried about him."

He just sat there for a second and thought about the time he had spent with Paul Kent twenty-five years ago.

"One day, he spoke about her and I asked him what had happened. All he knew was that she had just vanished from the face of the Earth soon after he had left the year they met."
Aaron looked at Lani.

"You know that the entire town has been in kind of a feud since Luana disappeared, right? The people who were on her and her Aunt Malani's side, and the people who were on Kumu Kalekilio's side. There are people who haven't shopped in his store for thirty years now, even though they probably don't even know why and they are the kids of the people who sided with Malani or Kumu." he had to laugh about that silliness.

"My big brother was friends with her and knew the entire story except the part about her going to Lanai. Malani and Luana's best friend Alana were the only ones who knew about that. Unfortunately, a few years after I had met him, my brother Peter told Paul in a conversation one day, that Luana had most likely been pregnant when she left. That made things much worse for Paul. Put him over the edge. He didn't seem to care about his own appearance anymore, always had a 3-day beard, wore torn clothes and seemed depressed.

He painted less and less and just spent all day looking for signs of Luana and her child while he was here during the summer. He always had a certain fixed date in late August when he had to leave and go back to the Thousand Islands, because he taught there at an art institute. That year, he was already at the airport, then changed his mind and decided to stay and keep searching for Luana. He even called his boss in New York and quit his job. And he actually called me to check on his regular cabin's availability. I always made the reservation for him. On his way back to Hana, the accident happened...."

In the meantime, a big sushi platter was served, with several sushi rolls, some sashimi and everything decorated with beautiful orchid blooms. Everyone oohed and aahed. It looked fantastic. But Lani sat quietly. She could not stop thinking about her poor, broken-hearted father.

She could barely eat anything, listening to this tragic story. She was hanging on Aaron's next words. Aaron took a brief break to have a piece of sushi, but didn't want to interrupt and continued, looking at Lani.

"So, did you know about the accident?"

"Yes, Max's friends in Lahaina told us about it. They just said that there was a mudslide and his car must have been pushed off of a cliff and that he was never found."

"Yeah, that's about it. He also could have just been tired. It was late and dark. I told him to stay overnight in Kahului or Paia, but he didn't want to. What a loss. He was a great guy."

"What I wonder about," said Lani. "is why it looks like everything about him has been removed from the internet. When you google him, there is nothing mentioned about his death and the accident. Don't you all find that strange?"

They all looked at each other. Yes, that was strange. Someone would have gone through a lot of trouble to get something like that removed.

"Well, I'm really sorry that I had such a sad story to tell you," Aaron said when they were finished with their meal, "but I'm very glad that we were all finally able to meet. Your Aunt Malani did the right thing to bring you here and I hope you decide to keep the house and stay."

Lani smiled. "Thank you, Aaron. And thanks for telling me about my dad. It's nice to know that he had great friends. I'm so glad I met you all too. And congrats on your sale today."

They all lifted their champagne glasses for a toast.

Chapter 43
Garden of Eden

It was already about three in the afternoon when Lani and Max finally left Mama's Fish House.

They'd still have plenty of time to get to Hana in daylight, but wouldn't be able to make many stops. Lani asked Max:

"I wanted to stop at Garden of Eden, because I'm interested in the plants there, do you think we'd have enough time to do at least that and would you mind?"

Max gave it some thought. "It's going to be tough, because they close at four. We could just go in really quick? We might not have more than forty minutes. But I don't know when you'll get another chance..."

"Okay, let's do it!" she replied.

He accelerated fast, even though a sharp curve was coming up. She gave him a strict look from the side that Max was already used to, and he grinned and slowed down significantly. They both smiled at each other.

"It's actually only a few miles to get there. I think it's located at about Mile Marker 10, just after a stand of rainbow eucalyptus trees. Can you help me keep an eye out for the entrance? It's right at a sharp curve, and I always drive by without noticing it."

And of course it happened: they both saw the entrance after they had almost passed it.

Lani yelled: "There it is!" and he had already driven by. He had to do a u-turn and that was not very easy on the road to Hana, which was also currently very busy. As soon as he saw a little sandy parking area on the side of the road, he turned onto that and waited for a break in the countless tourist cars and vans. He tried to do a u-turn as quickly as possible, but another oncoming car, that was driving a bit too fast, had already come around the curve and almost hit them. Almost. The driver, a local, had to break hard and had his hand pressed on the horn and wouldn't stop honking, until Max quickly spun the steering wheel around and accelerated to get out of the car's path. But he wasn't fast enough and the driver, who had the bigger momentum, passed them, which was a bit crazy on this road, and looked angrily into their car. Max immediately recognized his buddy Sam, who drove to Kahului on a regular basis to see his girlfriend, and started laughing. Sam recognized him too and was quite dumbfounded. They both stopped on the left at the entrance to the Garden of Eden and got out of their cars.

"Hey, what are you doing here, man, driving like a tourist?" Sam yelled at him, shaking his fist in a joking manner while he walked toward him and gave him a bear hug.

"Haha!" laughed Max. "Missed the entrance and had to turn around. Wasn't easy on this busy road."

"Hey, Lani!" said Sam, looking down into the car. "Maybe you should drive, I don't trust this guy! He drives worse than a tourist!" They all laughed and Sam got back into his car, waved and took off with squealing tires.

"Bye, guys! See y'all in Hana!" Sam yelled.

"Wow, do all of you locals drive this crazy?" Lani asked, laughing.

They drove up to the entrance of "Garden of Eden". The attendant in the little booth recognized Max and waved them through, since it was already so late.

"Thanks, man!" said Max and turned to Lani: "The benefits of being a local," he said with a grin.

They parked and walked across the parking lot where a bunch of ducks, geese and some peacocks immediately surrounded them, thinking Lani and Max had food for them. They shooed them away and walked onto a gravel walkway.

It was a beautiful botanical garden, filled with a big variety of tropical plants, lots of them in bloom. Lani enjoyed taking some time to check out the local plants. They continued to a shady walkway surrounded by various giant types of bamboo. Lani didn't know which way to continue, since there were various paths going into different directions like a maze and they hadn't bothered grabbing a map.

"Let's go to Puohokamoa Falls," said Max, pointing at a sign pointing to the right. "It's a really pretty waterfall that empties into a bigger pool and you have a really nice birds' eye view from here." They walked up the path leading to the viewpoint, saw the beautiful waterfall down below in the distance, but before they could even say anything, it suddenly started pouring!

"Let's find shelter somewhere. It will probably stop soon, but we don't want to get soaked," said Max and they ran past an empty parking lot toward a picnic area that was covered by a pergola. They were soaked within seconds. The rain was unusually hard and long for this time of year.

"I never thought about checking the weather. It's been so beautiful." said Max and pushed a strand of wet hair out of Lani's face. She stood there, shivering. It was actually quite chilly. He wrapped her in his arms to warm her up a bit and looked down at her. Their eyes met and seconds later, they stood there wrapped in a tight embrace, kissing each other. Lani did not feel chilled anymore. Quite the opposite.

When it finally stopped raining, it was past 4 pm, the garden was closed and everyone seemed to have left. The entire parking lot was empty except for Lani's car.

"Oh, boy," said Max. "I hope we can still get out of here and the gate isn't closed. I assume they must have seen our car and are still here, cleaning up…"

The air was so humid that steam was coming up from the asphalt in the parking lot. They were both entirely soaked and in this humidity it didn't look like their clothes would be drying anytime soon. They got some dry clothes out of their duffle bags in the trunk and quickly slipped into them behind the car. Then they got into the car and slowly drove up to the exit. With a sigh of relief, they realized that the gate was open. The attendant in the booth waved goodbye as they drove through the exit.

"Well, that was quite an adventure," said Lani as they turned onto the Hana Highway. It was starting raining again and, even though it was still in the afternoon, it was already quite dark on the highway, because of the low clouds and the heavy rain forest canopy.

Chapter 44

The windshield wipers were moving back and forth quickly, but Max still had a hard time seeing where he was driving. The rain was hard, the windshield kept fogging up and some of the many people coming toward him didn't realize that they had their brights on. It wasn't even dark yet, but everyone had their lights on early due to the hazardous road conditions. After a few miles, all traffic going both ways came to a sudden halt.

"There must have been an accident ahead of us," guessed Max.

"Oh, wow, that's quite scary. I hope nothing bad happened," replied Lani.

"This might take a while. We're almost at the Keanae Peninsula. If it moves a bit, we could stop there. Have you been there yet?"

"Yes, I stopped there on my first trip to Hana, but wouldn't mind stopping again. It was beautiful with the church, the rough ocean and the lava."

"There's a great coffee place down there with banana bread."

"Haha," replied Lani laughing. "Are you hungry again after that giant lunch?"

"I'm always hungry", said Max with a grin, "and that banana bread is worth it. We can take some home."

It felt so good how he spoke of "we" and "home"… That's exactly how Lani felt… She started thinking again…

Suddenly, the cars started moving again. It seemed that the cars involved in the accident had at least been pushed to the side of the road and others were able to pass, slowly, both sides having to take turns, because the road was so narrow. No ambulance or tow truck had passed them yet, but would have to come all the way from Paia. They slowly continued driving. They crossed a bridge and came up two cars that had obviously first crashed into each other and then into the guardrail. The occupants were all outside the cars and no one seemed to be seriously hurt.

"Wow, that's pretty bad," said Max, "I'm glad there's a guardrail here. Otherwise, they'd all be down there." He pointed down at the ocean that was at least a hundred feet below them.
Lani shuddered.

"I hope everyone is OK," Lani said, looking at the people sitting and standing on the side of the road. As a first responder, Max stopped briefly to check whether any more help was needed, but everything had been taken care of. Nobody needed an ambulance and a tow-truck for the car that was not driveable anymore was on its way.
Max asked: "Do you still want to stop and get the banana bread?"

"It's totally up to you! Isn't it getting dark soon?"

"I don't really mind driving in the dark, I'm used to it. You just won't have the pretty view anymore," replied Max.

"That's okay. I hope I can come back and stop at some of the scenic spots another time. Or on the way back when I leave..."

That hit a sore spot for both of them. Max glanced quickly at her without taking his eyes off of the road for too long. He realized that the turn down to the Keanae Peninsula was coming up and took a left onto the road that led down to the village. At a stand on the right, before the entrance of the village, Max stopped, got out and stretched his legs. Lani followed him. It had stopped raining in the meantime and it was nice and cool. As usual, everyone knew Max and greeted him with fist bumps and hugs and the lady behind the counter of the ramshackle banana bread stand, who could have been his mother, started flirting with him immediately. Lani grinned. In the meantime she understood why nobody could resist his charm...

They grabbed two cups of coffee and two loaves of banana bread (one for later) and walked across the street, down to an area where the waves crashed against the rugged black lava rock, with an incredible view of the beautiful coastline behind them that was all rain forest. They sat down on a big boulder, leaning against each other, and just watched the waves, while they enjoyed a piece of the fresh moist banana bread and held each other while the sun was slowly crawling lower and lower in the sky. It was already golden hour.

"We'd better get going," said Max and jumped up.

159

He took Lani's hand and pulled her up with so much momentum that she bumped into him and they just stood there again, looking into each other's eyes, hypnotized. They came to their senses and walked toward the car. It would be hard for Lani to leave in a few days.

It became dark quite soon, they still had half of the Road to Hana ahead of them, but Max knew his way back to Hana in his sleep. The road was nice and empty now. Most cars were already gone because people didn't want to drive in the dark and the light of the few oncoming cars was actually helpful in the curves and narrow areas. The beams of light showed Max ahead of time when a curve was coming up. They were both deep in their own thoughts and felt comfortable with each other and they just enjoyed the drive silently. Soon, they passed through Hana, took their usual route past Koki Beach and turned left into the driveway of Koki Beach House.

It felt like coming home to Lani, when she saw the pretty stately house in the moonlight and heard the ocean waves crashing.

Chapter 45

If Lani thought she and Max would have a nice relaxing evening and maybe just order a pizza and sit on the deck and have a beer or glass of wine, she was utterly disappointed.

There was a little sportscar parked in the driveway and, as soon as Max and Lani turned into the driveway, Mandy got out with a charming smile. She was wearing high heels, a short tanktop that showed off her curves and a tight mini skirt. She had obviously been waiting for Max.

"Wow, good luck with that," said Lani chilly, as they parked and got out of the car. She was beside herself and she felt like her head was about to explode, because her blood pressure was so high. This woman was quite persistent.

"It's not what you think it is. I seriously have no feelings for her." Max was beside himself too. He knew this looked odd, but he really didn't know what Mandy was doing here.

Lani grabbed her purse and got her duffle-bag out of the trunk and walked straight into the house, with a quick snarky "Hi, Mandy" in Mandy's direction.

Lani walked into the house and slammed the door shut.

"Oh, no, I'm sorry Maxi", said Mandy, walked up to him and gave him a kiss on the cheek. "I really didn't want to disturb you guys. We can still be friends, right, Maxi? Listen, some of Jill's family came over today surprisingly, and I have nowhere to stay and wondered if I could stay here, for just one night?"

"No. I'm sorry, I have to work tomorrow and I really can't let you stay here," he said, nodding toward the main house.

"But I won't bother you and it doesn't mean anything if I stay here. I just need a place to crash." she insisted.

"I'm sorry, Mandy, but it doesn't work that way. You can't just show up here and think you can stay overnight. Come on in. I'll make a couple of phone calls and see if there is anywhere else in town you can stay."

Of course, Lani was just looking out of the window to check whether Mandy had left already, when she saw Max and Mandy walking into the guesthouse together. She was fuming.

Max called several friends and the fire station's administrative assistant Jennifer actually really had a room that was available and that Mandy could use for the night.

"You are a lifesaver!", said Max. "I'll send her over. She should be there in about twenty minutes. Mahalo." And he hung up. He looked at Mandy.

"Okay, my colleague Jennifer's roommate just moved out and she has a room available. She lives on the other side of Hana, right past the fire station. You take a left onto Hana Highway where the road forks, then continue for about a quarter of a mile and take the first street to the right. Waikoloa Road. It's the second house on the left. Jennifer Gartner."

He grabbed a piece of paper and wrote down Jennifer's name and phone number.

"Here's her number in case you miss it. By the way, I thought you were leaving town the other day when you had the flat tire?"

"Ohhhh, I met this guy and was at a few parties with him… and I did want to say bye to you …" she looked up at him and batted her eyelashes. It didn't work though. He ushered her outside and said:

"Listen, I'm sorry, but I really have a lot to do and I have to work early tomorrow."

She finally gave up... "OK, have it your way… see you later, Maxi!"

"Bye."

Max walked over to the main house and rang the doorbell. He knew Lani was furious, but he wanted her to know as quickly as possible that this meant nothing. She was already in her pajamas when she opened the door and had a glass of wine in her hand.

"What's up? Did your girlfriend leave?"

He was a bit baffled that she was so confrontational.

"Come on, Lani. This wasn't my fault. And she is not my girlfriend. She didn't have a place to stay and I guess I was one of the few people she knows. I felt bad and found her a place to stay for the night."

Lani nodded. She hoped she could believe him. But she wanted to be alone and think about things.

"We're both tired. It's been a long day. Can we just call it a night?"

"Sure." He gave her a long look. "Can I say one more thing?"

She nodded.

"Aloha Wau la 'Oe'. That means: I love you."

He leaned forward and gave her a gentle kiss on the cheek. Then he turned around and disappeared in the guesthouse. She just stood there, touching her cheek. She just wanted to follow him out to the guesthouse, she was really in love with him. But she fought the urge. She couldn't. She didn't want to be hurt again...

Chapter 46

The next morning, Lani woke up quite late. In her frustration about the Mandy situation, she had drank one glass of wine too many and had quite a pounding headache.

Well, today I'm really going to take it easy, she thought, while she put her short Hawaii bathrobe on and shuffled over to the kitchen to make some coffee and get an alka-seltzer. She was glad that Max was probably already at work, because she didn't feel like running into him, although she had to keep thinking about what he had said to her last night. Maybe Mandy's behavior was really not his fault...

As she walked out onto the deck and sat down with her coffee, the phone rang. It was Max.

"Hello?' Lani answered the phone. She sounded a bit short.

"Hey, it's Max. How are you?"

"Actually not so great."

"I hope not because of Mandy? I promise you, she left town this morning. My coworker Jennifer told me. She was not too happy about having Mandy at her house, but she did me the favor."

"It's not because of Mandy," she lied, " I'm feeling a little under the weather. I'm just going to take it easy today."

"I wanted to let you know that the guys have their estimate done, as promised. They want to check out the wall in the guest room above the kitchen one more time and asked if they could come over later, around six. I'll be back from work by then too."

"Sure. I'll take a nap later and should be okay by then."

"Okay, thanks. Hope you feel better." said Max.

"Thanks," replied Lani, "see you later."

She ended the call.

While she was on the phone anyway, she decided to call Anne and her parents right away. It rang and rang in the flower shop and nobody picked up. That's strange, thought Lani to herself. It's about 4 pm New York time, you'd think she'd be in the shop right now. She tried Anne's cell phone. It rang and Anne picked up right away. She sounded like she was out of breath.

"Hi, Lani! It's so good to hear your voice! How are things going there?" she asked.

"Everything's okay, I just got back from Lanai, but not too much new information there, but I did find out a few more things about my father... not good though..."

"I'm sorry, Lani," Anne interrupted, "I'm going to have to call you back. We're having a bit of a situation here right now..."

"What's going on?" Lani asked worried.

"Remember when one of the sprinkler heads broke last year and the water came gushing out? The same thing happened again today. No emergency, Bill noticed it right away, because he just happened to be checking the greenhouses. He turned the water off. But Bill and I are carrying some of your orchids out of the way so that the repair guy can get up there with his ladder tomorrow morning and so that they don't get too water logged..."

"Oh no... and that has to happen while I'm not there! I'm so sorry about the extra work!" Lani was beside herself. "Can I talk to Bill? Is he there right now?"

"Yeah, hang on."

"Hey, Lani!" Bill said. "Really, don't worry about it right now. We'll have the affected area fixed tomorrow morning with a quick fix and when you're back, you can take care of a long-term solution."

"Meaning...?"

"Well, the sprinkler guy thinks you might have to renew the entire system in the orchid house in the long run."

Another unexpected major expense... Lani just sat there and stared at the beautiful ocean for a second. She felt as if she couldn't handle it all anymore. And then, in the midst of her nursery's expenses growing over her head, she was now trying to fix up this million Dollar house at the end of the world... what was she thinking?

"Lani, are you still there?"

"Yes, sorry Bill, I got distracted. I really really appreciate all your help."

Bill smiled. He loved helping Lani. Unfortunately, for a different reason, but he knew that Lani didn't return his feelings. He sighed, while they said goodbye, and ended the call. But in the next moment, he smiled at pretty Anne, who was working hard, carrying orchids to the other side of the greenhouse.

Chapter 47

Lani still had a bit of a headache and took a long nap with the sound of the waves in the background. When she woke up, it was already noon, but she felt much better. She stretched. Whatever decisions she would have to make, she was thankful to be here in this beautiful paradise and to have met all the wonderful people.

She grabbed her phone and called Phillip at Maui Exotics.

"Aloha! Maui Exotics, this is Phillip!"

"Hi, Phillip, it's Lani. I wanted to stop by this afternoon and look for a plant to ship to one of my friends in New York. Are you going to be around?"

"Oh, yes, I will. I'll be quite busy, but I'll be glad to help you. We received an orchid shipment from Honolulu this morning. There's a lot to unpack. I'm sure you'd love to see the orchids. I ordered some really nice Cattleya species and a bunch of new hybrids."

"That IS exciting! I'd love to come over and help for a while!" Lani replied, full of excitement.

"Okay, I'll see you then."

"It's twelve now, I'll see you around two?"

"Perfect. See you later."

"Bye."

Lani looked at her watch. She had two hours until she was going over to Maui Exotics, so she had enough time to go to the beach and then have lunch at one of the food trucks.

She quickly changed into her swimsuit, grabbed a towel, sunscreen, a cereal bar, a bottle of water and some fruit that she had already cut up and put these items into a big beachbag.

The short walk to Hamoa Beach was beautiful as usual, she walked about one hundred yards down the paved road and already had the most beautiful bird's eye view onto the postcard-perfect crescent shaped beach that was surrounded by cliffs. The turquoise-colored ocean was sparkling in the sun and the fronds of the palm trees were swaying in the gentle breeze. As she walked past the big plumeria trees right behind the low stone wall on the oceanside of the road, she picked up one of the flowers and stuck it behind her ear. In this moment, she was happy and carefree. With her slight tan that made her skin glow and her dark straight hair, she looked like a true local.

She walked down the stairs that led to the beach and over to her regular spot in the sand under the palm trees where she put her beach bag onto the rocks on the edge of the beach. The sand felt warm and soft under her feet. She stood there for a second checking out the waves. The water was cold at first, but it felt refreshing after walking in the hot sun. She just went for a dip and then returned to her spot under the trees to relax in the shade.

A younger couple with two little children about three and five years old came down to the beach and set up a little tent to provide shade for the kids. After applying sunscreen on the kids that squealed in protest, they all ran down to the water and Lani enjoyed watching them play in the surf for a while. The little children screamed when the small waves hit them and ran back ashore. When they had enough of that, they got some sandtoys out and started building a sand castle, content and relaxed. Lani smiled. It was really like paradise.

She checked the time on her phone. It was time to leave if she wanted to stop for lunch at the Huli Huli chicken food truck or the Thai food truck in Hana.

She gathered up her things and washed the sand off of her feet at the shower. Then she looked back at the beach and the little family one more time and walked up the stairs and back to the house. She felt happy and refreshed.

Chapter 48

Lani got in her car, stopped at the Thai food truck for lunch. Then she drove a few miles out of Hana. The butterflies started fluttering again in her stomach when she drove past the fire station and saw Max's truck parked in front of the building.

She took a left into the long driveway leading to Maui Exotics. She really hoped she'd find a really nice ginger plant for Bill, who had been helping so much, and have it shipped to him as a gift.

Phillip and two of his assistants were very busy. They had just received the big shipment from Blue Tropics Orchids in Honolulu that Phillip had told Lani about. Some of the orchids were even blooming, so they were all meticulously wrapped in newspaper and bubble-wrap, some of the more sensitive blooms had even been thoughtfully protected with cotton balls and had to be unwrapped very carefully to not be damaged. Some were bareroot seedlings and divisions and would have to be potted soon. Even though these orchids were not for Lani, it felt like Christmas unwrapping and looking at each beautiful plant that came out of one of the boxes.

While Lani was pulling a piece of newspaper off of an orchid, something attracted her attention. She stopped, set the orchid down, smoothed out the piece of newspaper and took a closer look. It was a page of a newspaper from a small town right outside of Honolulu, Palolo Valley. Am I imagining things, she thought to herself.

She took a closer look at the article. It was an older newspaper and the article featured the same nursery that this shipment was from: Blue Tropics Orchids. They had won several prizes at an orchid show in Honolulu. What had caught Lani's attention was the photo of the owners of the nursery and their employees, standing lined up in front of a wall full of paintings. One of the paintings on the wall was a small painting of Luana. The photo was quite grainy, but Lani recognized it. It was definitely a Paul Kent painting!

Lani took a closer look at the people in the photo. They were a bit blurry, since the photo was so small and the newspaper was already quite wrinkly and torn. It was a middle-aged couple, the nursery owners, surrounded by several younger employees. The woman was Hawaiian and the man an older Caucasian. Lani thought it might be Luana! She showed it to Phillip.

"Phillip, can you take a look at this photo. Do you know the people at this nursery? Look at this painting and this woman! Don't you think this could be Luana?! Have you ever met this woman at one of the shows?"

"Hmmm…." replied Phillip. "I can't really recognize the woman very well. I guess it could be her… I've met Patrick a few times at orchid shows, but his wife never comes, so I've never met her…"

"Of course the woman would be thirty years older, but have you ever seen any of the older paintings of her? I'm pretty sure that's her in the painting. Of course it still might not mean the woman in this photo is the woman in the painting…"

Phillip got his reading glasses out of his pocket, took the piece of newspaper and studied the people in the photo as well as the painting in the back.

"I do agree that it looks like a painting of Luana. But I can't recognize the woman."

"Do you mind if I keep this article?" asked Lani.

"No, of course not," Phillip replied with a smile. "Actually, you can take this too. Thanks for helping with the shipment."

He handed her the orchid that Lani had just unwrapped.

"Awww. Thank you Phillip! I love this one!" she gave him a spontaneous hug.

After being so happy and carefree unpacking the orchids, Phillip could feel how tense Lani was now, thinking of her mother and obsessing about having to find her. Even though he understood, he tried to distract her and change the subject.

"Why don't we go and look for a plant for your friend now," he proposed.

"Yes, good idea," Lani replied. It's getting late and I have to meet some handymen at the house at six."

They walked to the outside area of the nursery that consisted of rows and rows of tropical plants such as ginger, heliconia, hibiscus, birds of paradise, small types of bamboo, small palm trees and many more.

"Choose a nice-sized plant, shipping is not as much as you think," said Phillip, "look at these ti-plants. Their leaves are just gorgeous." They continued walking through the rows. "Or this awapuhi ginger, also called pine cone ginger. You can squeeze the liquid from the cone and wash your hands or hair with it. That would be quite an unusual and special gift. And they grow like a weed, so he'll be able to divide them soon and sell them. Didn't you say it's for a co-worker?"
Lani clapped her hands and smiled at him.

"That's perfect, Phillip! That's actually what he had mentioned! Yes, he owns a nursery as well. He'll love it."
They chose a nice-sized plant and Phillip carried it up to the office where it would be properly packaged with heat packs, since it was going to a colder region, and shipped the next day.

"The plant is a gift from me," said Phillip. "How about you pay for shipping. I won't know how much that is until tomorrow. My assistant Nali will pack it in a box and weigh it tomorrow."

"Phillip, you don't have to do that," said Lani. "You're giving me too much!" "It's fine," answered Phillip with a smile. "I'm considering it an investment, since I'd like you to work with me when you come back."

"You never know," replied Lani. "It sure would be fun to work here."

Chapter 49

As soon as Lani had left and was on her way back to Koki Beach House, her brain started racing. She had to go to Palolo Valley, which was outside of Honolulu, and see if that woman in the photo was her mother. As soon as she was home, she was going to check on flights. She looked at the clock in her car. It was already five thirty, helping in the nursery had taken longer than expected. Max and his two friends were going to be at her house in thirty minutes. She stopped at the food truck at Koki Beach and got a few portions of Huli Huli chicken, an easy meal, in case they stayed for dinner and if they didn't stay, it was good for leftovers. As soon as she stopped in the driveway, a truck drove up behind her. Keanu and Billy were already here. Max's truck was also already in the driveway. She walked up to the truck and greeted Keanu and Billy.

"Aloha, guys, thanks for coming. I got some Huli Huli chicken. Do you want to discuss your estimate over dinner?"

"Aloha, Lani! That's super nice of you, but Alana is barbecuing tonight and I have to be back by 7:30," replied Billy. Keanu already had plans as well and declined.

"Well, I guess I'm going to have Huli Huli chicken for a week then," Lani replied laughing.

"Don't worry, I'm right here and I love Huli Huli chicken," Max said grinning. He had heard them arrive and was just stepping up behind Lani.

Keanu and Billy laughed.

"Oh, you don't have to worry about that guy's appetite!" said Keanu with a grin.

Lani and Max joined in with the laughter, Lani not so heartily. Even though Lani seemed a bit distanced from Max, he stole a quick peck on her cheek, which she didn't really know how to react about, because she was still a bit upset about Mandy.

They all walked into the house and sat down at the kitchen table. Billy put a manila folder on the table that he had been holding in his hand. Lani got some beers out of the fridge and brought them over to the table.

"Thanks!" said Max, Keanu and Billy. They opened their beers, clinked the bottles and said "cheers!"

"I don't know what you guys were expecting or if you have to stay under any certain number, but here's the bad news," said Billy. He pushed the manila folder across the table toward Lani and opened it. The top page was an Excel spreadsheet.

"It's right under 95 grand. That includes the new roof for both the main building and the guesthouse, an entirely new wooden deck and new vanities for the master bathroom. Take your time and look at it. I'm sure we can tweak a few things," continued Billy. Lani had expected a quite extensive amount, but she was still a bit shocked to see it black on white. She looked through the pages of the estimate, which seemed to be put together very professionally. There was an estimate for every single item from a home improvement or hardware store.

"So, this includes labor and materials?" she asked.

"Yes, it includes everything," replied Billy. "But it's really not a firm number, since we really have to take a second closer look at the house, for example, we need to take another look at the wall on the west side of the house which has all the water damage. We need to check if it affects the second story at all and measure the entire wall again. I mean, we can't guarantee that nothing else shows up while we're working…" Lani nodded. She understood.

"Let's go and check out that wall," said Max and they all got up, Keanu and Billy grabbed two tape measures and they all walked upstairs. While they were all in the big guestroom facing the guesthouse, knocking against the wall and checking out how far up the water damage had soaked the wood and the men were chit-chatting and joking in their usual boisterous manner, Lani realized that there was a small crawl space on each side of the room under the roof that opened up with a little wooden latch, which she hadn't noticed before. The wooden latches weren't bigger than a popsicle stick, and the small door leading to the crawl space was barely distinguishable from all the other wood. She kneeled down and pushed the small latch sideways and tried to open the door. It was stuck from not being opened for years. She couldn't open it with her fingers or finger nails and had to ask the men for a tool.

"Guys, there's a door here that I can't open with my bare hands. Do you have a screw-driver or something long and thin like that up here?" They looked up. They didn't, but Keanu ran downstairs to get one. In the meantime, Billy and Max walked over to where Lani was standing and tried to pry the door open with their fingers. They couldn't open it either and had to wait for Keanu. Keanu arrived with a scraper and a screwdriver. The scraper wasn't strong enough and just broke off, so he stuck the tip of the screwdriver into the side of the door and jimmied it open. The door finally popped open and they discovered a folded up easel, old art supplies, paints and chemicals, empty canvasses. In the way back, behind everything, Lani spied something else behind the art supplies. She started pulling out the old supplies and had to crawl deeper into the crawl space that she barely fit into, to be able to reach the items in the back.

Fire fighter Max looked into the crawl space and saw all of the chemicals and turpentine bottles and said:

"Wow, this is quite the fire hazard," he said from the back, while he took the items that she was handing him from the dark and dusty hole in the wall. Malani must have stored Paul Kent's or someone else's painting supplies up here. There were a ton of old dried up oil paints, old rusty bottles of turpentine and other paint thinners, boxes of brushes and old canvasses, some still wrapped in plastic. Finally, Lani, who couldn't turn around in the tight space, came crawling backwards carefully, supporting herself with her elbows, while she was holding something up in her hands. It was obviously a few smaller canvasses, but these had been wrapped carefully in a blanket. Lani came out, she was covered in dust and had to sneeze. She unwrapped the blanket from the canvasses, and they all laid eyes on some beautiful little square paintings in about 16 x 16 inches that seemed to be from Paul Kent! It was definitely his style and, yes, they also had his signature!

"Wow!" said Lani. "And luckily, the water damage doesn't seem to have come up this far, right, men?"

They nodded. Indeed, they hadn't found any water damage up here in the second floor.

"The paintings look like they're still in good shape," said Lani. She looked at the paintings, one by one. It was six of them. They were beautiful landscapes, two were Iao Valley, one seemed to be Honolua Bay, two were Red Sand Beach from two different angles and the last one was another painting of beautiful Hamoa Beach.

"It almost seems like I was meant to find these to help with the renovation, but then on the other hand, who would want to sell these? They're so beautiful," Lani said, looking at the paintings.

"Yes, they are," replied Max. "What a find. I wonder if Malani forgot about them. They must be pretty valuable," he added.

Keanu and Billy were done with their work and had just hung out out of curiosity.

"Well, we need to get going," said Billy. "Take a closer look at the estimate and let us know if there's anything we should add or take out."

"Thanks for all your hard work so far," said Lani. She couldn't imagine how she would ever be able to afford all these repairs and renovations.

It was a bit awkward to be alone with Max, but Lani thought she might as well use up the Huli Huli chicken.

"Would you like some of the tons of Huli Huli chicken I bought, because I thought those guys might stay for dinner?"

"Sure, I'd love some," replied Max.

Lani unwrapped the Huli Huli chicken and they both decided that it was still warm enough to eat. They sat down on the back deck with two more beers.

"Lani, I'm really sorry. This whole Mandy thing is just really such a bad coincidence. There's seriously nothing going on between us and, as far as I'm concerned, she won't be returning."

"My ex-boyfriend cheated on me with a blonde, who is now his girlfriend. I might be overreacting a bit, but this whole Mandy situation reminds me of that," Lani answered.

"Oh no," replied Max. He looked at her across the table with his dark brown eyes. "Forget about Mandy. Lani, I love you. I mean it."

"Just give me some time, please. I don't know what to do right now. There are so many crazy things happening. The house. Coming here. Meeting you. Our trip to Lanai. And now the paintings… and this." She got up and got the newspaper article out of her purse and showed it to him. He looked at it and nodded. "Wow! Do you think that's her?"

"You can't really recognize her, the photo is too grainy, but look at the painting in back of the people… that's definitely one of the Paul Kent paintings…"

She asked "Are there flights from Hana to Honolulu? I really think I have to go there."

He nodded and replied "There are flights from Hana, but they all stop in Kahului. So, it's really up to you if you want a four hour flight that stops in Kahului without the drive or a 45 minute flight after driving to Kahului. It's six of one, half dozen of the other… But remember, you only have four or five more days until you leave, so there's not much time left. That would take at least a full day and you may even have to stay overnight in Honolulu. You could always save that for your next trip or change your return flight and fly back through Honolulu."

"I think I have to go now, I can't stop thinking about it. I'll check on flights later."

They were done with dinner and Max decided to give her some space, so he got up to leave. He was now standing next to Lani, looked down in her eyes, took her face gently in his palms and gave her a kiss on the lips.

"Good night, Lani. I hope you can decide to believe me."

She really wanted to believe him, but with the way Mandy kept showing up, she just wasn't sure… She needed some time alone to think about things... As soon as Max had left and she heard the door of the guesthouse being opened and shut, Lani opened up her laptop and checked on flights from Hana to Honolulu and, in comparison, from

Kahului to Honolulu. Since she'd be going by herself, she decided to fly directly from Hana and save the long drive to Kahului on the Hana Highway. She could just sit in the plane and relax. It would also probably be fun to fly along Maui's coastline in a small plane. She found a seat on the cheapest flight for the day after tomorrow at 10 am, arriving in Honolulu at 2 pm and returning to Hana on Thursday, the next day, in the early evening. That way she'd have about 24 hours in Honolulu and she'd have two and a half more days left in Hana before her flight home on Sunday evening.

After that, she reserved a rental car for one day in Honolulu and started looking for a hotel. She was so excited, that she couldn't sleep. Not only because of possibly finding her mother, but also going to a big nursery outside of Honolulu. And a big city like Honolulu would be a totally different experience than sleepy Hana too.

Chapter 50

The next morning, the ringing of her phone woke Lani up. It was Aaron, who had heard through the locals' grapevine about the paintings Lani had found in the crawl space and wanted to see them as soon as possible. Obviously Billy had told Alana and Alana had told him. He cut right to the chase.

"Hey Lani. How are you?"

"Great! Good morning, Aaron!"

"Hey, Alana told me that you found some of Paul Kent's paintings in the house. I talked to her this morning, because I'm driving over to the gallery in Hana Hotel today. I happen to have a friend visiting from Los Angeles, who's an art appraiser and Alana wants us to come and look at some paintings she's commissioning for the gallery. We would love to come and also see your paintings if you're available. Could you meet us at the gallery? I'd love to see them."

Lani was hesitant.

"I'm not sure if I want to sell them though…"

"That doesn't matter. I'd just love to see them, and my friend William can estimate their value. That wouldn't hurt, even if just for insurance purposes."

"Hmmm… good idea. Okay, no problem. I'd love to see you too," Lani replied. "When are you arriving in Hana?"

"I'm meeting Alana at noon. Do you want to meet us there at the same time or can we come over to your place afterwards? I've actually only seen the big painting of Luana once years ago – I'd love to see it again… We could bring something for lunch…"

Lani remembered the Huli Huli chicken and chuckled.

"I don't know if you like chicken salad, but I have a ton of chicken I bought last night – I could make a chicken salad and I have a ton of fruit here - and maybe you could bring some nice fresh bread from the store?"

"That sounds perfect! We eat out so much that I'd love some homemade chicken salad. We'll bring something for dessert too."

"Okay! How long will you be at Alana's? An hour?"

"Probably just half an hour. Let's say we'll be at your house at 1:00."

"Okay," replied Lani. "I'm looking forward to seeing you."

"Can you please text me the address again, just in case I don't remember which house it is?"

"Sure."

"See you soon."

"Drive careful."

They ended the call and Lani texted Aaron her street address. She had to smile. There was one thing about Hana: you never stayed alone for a long time, even if you wanted to. She had been looking forward to a nice lazy day again, but she also loved the company, and Aaron was a nice guy. She had also wanted to go and check on her grandmother in the hospital, but she could do that afterwards in the afternoon. She looked at the time on her phone. It was eight-thirty, so she still had some time to have a nice breakfast on the deck and maybe go for a quick swim afterwards and then make chicken salad. She walked over to the fridge to check whether she had all the ingredients. Thank goodness, she had bought a jar of mayonaise just the other day. She also had apples and pickles and knew there were some Maui onions growing in the yard. That was all that she needed for her mother Lynn's chicken salad recipe.

She walked out into the yard with a sharp knife and looked for a couple of onion stalks and pulled them out of the ground. Then she walked over to a bigger pineapple plant and cut the pineapple off right at the bottom of the fruit, making sure she didn't scratch herself on the prickly plant. In the meantime, she had a hard time carrying everything, but she made it back to the kitchen without dropping anything and unloaded the treasures from the garden. She twisted the green crown off of the pineapple and put it out on the porch to dry in the sun. In a couple of days she was going to stick it back into the ground and a new pineapple plant would grow.

After having a nice breakfast on the deck, she remembered the mess that the men and she had left upstairs yesterday in front of the crawl space. So she ditched her idea to go to the beach for now, grabbed a vacuum cleaner, some rubber gloves, a bucket with soapy water and a garbage bag and walked upstairs to clean up the paint supplies instead. She vacuumed the entire area outside of the crawl space. Then she started throwing the old dried up paints that were at least twenty to twenty-five years old into the garbage bag. She couldn't throw all the chemicals like the turpentine away, they probably needed to go to a special hazardous waste disposal, so she walked down to the garage and looked for a box that she could put all the bottles into. To her surprise, there actually seemed to still be liquid in some of the bottles after all this time. While Lani was putting the bottles and jars into the box, one of the old bottles broke, and Lani had to quickly run and get a roll of paper towel to wipe up the thick liquid that smelled disgusting and made her cough. She set the box and the paper towels aside.

She turned the vacuum cleaner on one more time and pushed it ahead of her into the deep crawl space. Suddenly, she bumped against something with the vacuum cleaner brush that she seemed to have pushed deeper into the space and must have overlooked yesterday. She wondered if it was another flatter painting that she hadn't noticed yesterday, got her phone and turned the flashlight on, while she crawled back inside.

She discovered a big flat manila envelope and picked it up. It had the name *LUANA* written on it with big letters. It must have been wrapped up in between the paintings and fallen out yesterday. Lani crawled out backwards, sat down and opened up the envelope. She had discovered an unbelievable treasure. The envelope was full of thirty-year old photos of her mother and father, some black and white, some color, from the one summer they had spent together. Most of them were portraits of Luana, posing in various locations, each one seemingly more beautiful than the other, but some of them were also of Paul Kent and both of them, which a third person must have taken in various areas of Maui. Lani was sitting on the floor and had tears running down her cheeks while she looked at them. There weren't any pictures of her father on the internet and she was seeing photos of him for the first time. What a handsome man he was and what a beautiful couple they had been... She sat there for a while and totally forgot about what she had been doing, until she realized that she must have totally lost track of time. She looked at the clock on her phone: It was already noon! She gathered up the photos, pushed them back into the envelope, left everything else the way it was and rushed downstairs to make the chicken salad.

She put the envelope in a safe spot on the kitchen counter and started chopping chicken, onions, apples and pickles. She also added some walnuts that she had bought the other day as a snack. Then she added enough mayonnaise to make the salad nice and creamy. She cut up the pineapple, papaya and some melon she had in the fridge and put the fruit on a nice tray. As soon as she had pushed the tray and the bowl back into the fridge, someone knocked at the door.

It was Aaron and his friend William, a tall distinguished looking man with salt and pepper hair in his late forties to early fifties.

"I'm sorry, gentlemen, I'm a mess," she said, while she shook their hands. "I just found something upstairs and totally lost track of time. Would you like something to drink, while I go and freshen up a little for a few minutes?" She had a better idea:

"– Or why don't you take a look at the big painting of Luana in the great room? Come on in."

"Honey, don't worry, you look gorgeous as usual," said Aaron. "You'd even look gorgeous in rags... I'm sorry that we're intruding on you like this. Lunch would have really not been necessary..."

"No worries, I just got totally distracted, but I'll show you what I found in a few minutes – I'll be right back."

She led Aaron and William, who were curious now, to the great room, pointed at the painting and got them each a glass of water. Then she rushed upstairs to wash her face and her hands and comb her hair.

She walked back downstairs and greeted the two men again, who were still standing in front of the big painting of Luana at Hamoa Beach. As soon as William saw Lani, he started oohing and aahing about the painting.

"Wait until I show you what I found today, the reason why my face is so blotchy from crying. I'm still speechless."

She walked over to the kitchen counter and waved at the two men to follow her.

She took out the photos of Luana and Paul Kent and spread some of them out on the counter. Aaron and William were speechless. They stared at the never-seen-before beautiful photos of young Luana in her tropical paradise as well as some great portraits of Paul Kent and the couple together, and their jaws dropped. If Lani let them release these photos to the public, they were going to be a sensation. Paul Kent had not only been a great painter, but also a great photographer and this fact was pretty much unknown to the world.

"Wow, Lani, if you let us publicize these photos as well as the paintings, we could all make a lot of money. You wouldn't even have to sell the paintings, they could just go on tour for a while."

Lani walked over to her bedroom and got the six paintings she had found last night and showed them to the two men.

"These are amazing. Just beautiful." said William. "Just one of these is probably worth at least five thousand dollars."

Lani felt a little light-headed. She didn't know if it was from hearing all of these big amounts or because she was so hungry.

"I'm really sorry, I just realized how hungry I am. You two must be starving after coming all the way from Paia…"

Aaron hit his forehead with his hand. "Oh, I forgot the bread and the cake in the car. And it's so hot out. I'll be right back…"

Lani quickly set the table and got the chicken salad and fruit out of the fridge, while Aaron came inside with a loaf of French baguette, some multigrain bread and a delicious looking cake. Lani put the cake in the fridge, sliced the bread and took it outside in a pretty basket. For a while, they ate with a great appetite and just enjoyed the beautiful surroundings and the company.

"This is such a nice place," said Aaron. "We'll have to walk down to Hamoa Beach after lunch. I'd love to show it to William."

"Sure," replied Lani. "I'd actually love to go for a swim. I got really sweaty dusting and vacuuming upstairs in that tight crawl space where I found the paintings and the photos. Did you bring your bathing suits, by any chance?" she asked.

"Yes, we did. How can you go on the Road to Hana and not bring a bathing suit?" replied Aaron and winked at Lani who blushed, because she had done it before…

****

After having coffee and some of the delicious lilikoi chiffon pie, they all changed into their bathing suits and walked down to the beach. It was a beautiful day with some light showers in between that didn't even bother them. William was amazed by the stunning views and the beautiful perfectly crescent-shaped beach. They all dropped their things on the rocks underneath some trees in the shade and walked straight into the waves that were a bit stormier today and bodysurfed like teenagers. Another beautiful day in paradise.

After a while, they all had cooled off enough and sat on the beach, pondering about life, but they quickly got back to Luana and Paul Kent's love affair in this exact spot thirty years ago.
Especially Aaron, who had been Paul Kent's student and friend, couldn't stop thinking of him and the new paintings Lani had found.

"Lani, I would really love to have a Paul Kent exhibit in my gallery, if you would lend me the paintings and photos. It can be small, but I'm sure it will have a great reception. I also have a friend in Honolulu who I'm sure would love to exhibit the photos with some selected paintings in his gallery too. It's really a less known fact that Paul Kent was a great photographer too. We could seriously create a touring exhibit, and you could make some money with that…"

Lani nodded. "I don't see why we shouldn't show these photos to the world, but I'm not sure how my mother would think about it, if she was still alive…. She might be living somewhere with a different name. I'm really not sure what to think… I'm actually flying to Honolulu tomorrow. I found a photo in an old newspaper article about a nursery in Honolulu, which could possibly be hers. It also looks like, just by coincidence, there's a painting of her in the background of the photo… Also, regarding Paul Kent's paintings and photos, I guess we'd have to check if there are any other relatives of his alive and whether they'd claim any rights…"

"Wow! I hope you find her, Lani," replied Aaron. "And true about Paul Kent, although I don't think he had any other family. And I know for a fact he was a single child and his parents were quite old… Let us know if you find any new leads in Honolulu."

"Sure and I'll let you know. By the way, guys, I still had plans to go and visit my grandmother in the hospital this afternoon. I'm going to get going, if that's okay with you. I think it must be around 3:30 already," while she fumbled in her beachbag, looking for her phone. "Feel free to use the upstairs shower in the house, the downstairs bathroom is currently not usable. The house needs a lot of work…"
Aaron and William looked at each other.

"We should get going too", replied Aaron and got up. "I don't really like to drive in the dark. If we leave here at four without making any stops, we won't be back in Paia until six, and I wanted to stop at my brother Peter's stand."
William nodded, jumped up as well and they all gathered up their belongings, showered the sand off at the little shower by the exit of the beach and walked back to the house.

"We don't need to shower," said Aaron, who was in quite a rush now. "The shower down at the beach was enough and who knows if we end up jumping into one of the waterfalls on the way. It's too tempting…."
"Thanks for the delicious lunch, Lani, and let's stay in touch," said Aaron.

"Yes, thanks for lunch, and it was nice to meet you," added William.

"Thanks for coming, guys. It was nice to meet you, William."
Lani gave Aaron a hug and shook William's hand.

Chapter 51

As soon as Aaron and William had left, Lani jumped into the shower and got ready to go to the hospital.

Lani got into her car and drove the short picturesque drive to Hana Community Hospital. She drove really slowly past the general store, because she wanted to try and see whether Kumu was in the store or not. She was pretty sure he'd have to be there, since Leila was out of commission, but she couldn't see much from her point of view. I hope I don't run into him at the hospital, she thought to herself. I really don't know what to say to him...

When Lani knocked and stepped into Leila's room, Leila was just getting ready to go for a short exercise walk with the assistance of a young nurse and a walker.

"Aloha, you're right on time," said the nurse and smiled at Lani. "Leila's husband was supposed to come and help her with her walk, but he had to cancel. It was too busy in the store. Maybe you could just keep an eye on her while she walks and make sure she doesn't overdo it or fall?"

"Of course," replied Lani, as she walked up to Leila, greeted her and then quickly found a big vase that she filled with water and placed the flowers into.

"Mahalo for coming my child... and mahalo for the beautiful flowers," said Leila. Her eyes filled up with tears. She became very emotional when she saw her grandchild who reminded her of her daughter so much.

Lani stepped up to her grandmother, put her hand gently around her shoulder, supporting her a bit and helped her walk the few steps into the hallway.

"Sure, Grandmother." They both looked at each other surprised that Lani had automatically called Leila "Grandmother". Leila stopped and looked at her with a smile.

"Please call me Tutu," she said. "Grandmother in Hawaiian. I'm so thankful that I'm getting to know you in my old days, my child. My prayers have been answered. You remind me so much of your mother."

Lani smiled and nodded. "Let's walk a few more steps," she said. "We want you to get better soon."

Lani could tell that it was hard for Leila to walk, but that she was trying hard. They walked slowly up and down the hallway, Leila leaning into the walker and with Lani's arm around her shoulder. Lani felt like she had known her grandmother forever and told her about her nursery in the Hudson Valley and her two Basset Hounds.

"Your mother loved plants too, especially orchids," said Leila. "She used to help out at Maui Exotics a lot. Her dream was to go to college in Honolulu and become a landscape designer or to have her own nursery like Maui Exotics one day."

The picture of Blue Tropics Orchids in Honolulu came to Lani's mind, but she didn't want to mention it yet.

As soon as they were about to step back into the room, Kumu came up the hallway and saw them laughing, immersed in a nice conversation. He stopped, watched them disappear in the room and felt that he would disturb them and turned around and walked away, sadly, with his head hanging low. What could he do to make Lani forgive him too?

Chapter 52

When Lani returned to the beach house, she could see that Max was home, because his truck was there. One of the surfboards was missing which meant he was down at the beach, surfing.

Lani really would have loved to go down to the beach and surf with Max, but on the other hand, she really wanted to be alone and just think about things. She had to look over the estimate for the house one more time and hadn't even had a chance to really look at the photos of the people who were most likely her biological parents. Once again, the she had missed the chance to call Lynn and Mark. Due to the time difference, it was already too late in the Hudson Valley and they were probably asleep.

She planned on making herself a very simple meal with spaghetti and meat sauce and some tomatoes and mozzarella, but first she wanted to go outside to see if she could find any basil in the overgrown herb and vegetable garden next to the house.

She got a bit distracted and walked through the yard, down to the ocean and sat on the old swing for a while, just looking out at the roaring waves that hit the lava rock with that sound that she found both musical and meditative. The ocean put her at peace and she looked into the distance toward Alau Island that stuck out of the ocean like a dark shark's fin and thought about her life in the Hudson Valley and how this house here would possibly uproot everything she had been planning on doing in her life. This was truly paradise though. Regardless of what happened between her and Max, she could seriously imagine living here and continuing the legend that her great-aunt Malani had created. Everyone knew Koki Beach House as a place of big events, parties and happiness, especially the children of Hana. This had obviously filled a void in Malani's life, because she didn't have children of her own…

Suddenly, Lani spotted a Honu, a green sea turtle. This one seemed a bit smaller than the ones she had seen in Ho'okipa Beach Park and she wasn't even sure if they were usually sighted on this side of the island.

Lani wasn't really an extremely spiritual person, but she wondered if this Honu was a sign.

"Are you lost, my friend?" she asked the turtle, but then she had to laugh at herself because she was talking to a turtle. He was just lying there, in a little sandy spot in between the lava boulders, resting. She watched him for a while, but then she felt how hungry she was and looked back at the trees and plants in the yard. She turned around and looked for the Honu one more time, but he was gone. She got up and walked through the garden. It was golden hour and everything was dipped into a beautiful light and seemed warmer and softer than usual.

Lani made a quick dinner with meat sauce and spaghetti, some mozzarella and some fresh basil and tomatoes from the yard, cleaned up and still had a bit of cabin fever. She saw the light in the guesthouse and, to distract herself, she decided to call Alana and ask if she wanted to go and have a drink at the Hana Hotel. Billy was in Kahului for a few days, and Alana was more than happy to meet at the bar of Hana Hotel.

Lani arrived at Hana Hotel and stepped into the bar, when she received a text message from Alana that she was going to be about ten minutes late and to go ahead and order a drink. Lani went ahead and sat down at the corner of the bar where she could overlook the entire room and greeted the bartender, who was one of Max's friends and she had met the last time they had been there. They chatted for a while, but then the bartender had to take care of some other guests. Lani looked through the room. It was quite late already and the bar had already emptied out. Suddenly, a man stepped into the bar, the middle-aged heavyset man that had stared at her a few times and who was obviously the investor who wanted to buy Koki Beach House: Joseph McAllen. He walked up to Lani and, without even asking, he sat down a bit too close to her for comfort.

"May I?" he asked a bit too late. He had a very loud voice and acted as if he might have already been drinking. "What a way to end a nice evening, sitting next to such a gorgeous young lady..."

Lani didn't know how to reply and felt cornered. She scooted a bit to the side to have some more personal space. She was about to get up and sit down somewhere else.

"Aren't you the young lady who's staying at Koki Beach House?" Lani nodded, hesitantly.

"I don't think it's worth fixing up that old shack, do you? For less money you can bulldoze the place and build something brand new and shiny, like some nice condos…"

Lani was frozen. She felt very uncomfortable. Thank goodness, in this instance, Alana came up and rescued her. She interrupted the obnoxious man.

"Hey, Lani. Sorry to be late. Grab your drink and let's go over to one of the tabletops. It's more comfortable over there."

Alana didn't have to say that twice. Lani grabbed her drink and purse, nodded at the barkeeper, who had already noticed how unpleasant Joseph was and nodded back, jumped up and followed Alana to the other side of the room.

Lani set down her drink on a round hightop and gave Alana a hug.

"Oh, boy, you saved me. That guy is creepy," said Lani. "I almost regretted coming here."

"I'm really sorry to be so late. I was watching my daughter's two kids and she came home a bit late."

"Awww. I didn't know you're a grandmother already," Lani replied. "Do you have any photos of them?"

Alana got her mobile phone out and looked through her photos. Of course, it didn't take her very long to find photos of her grandchildren, because that's what most of her photos were. She showed Lani:

"The older one is five and a boy. His name is Billy Jr., and the younger one is 3 and her name is Malia. They are wild, but they keep me in shape."

"Oh, they are adorable. You must be so proud of them."

In this instance, Joseph walked by, stopped at the table and leaned on it so hard that it almost tipped over. He said:

"Well, I'm going to get that house, I just know it. I usually get what I want."

He attempted to pound his fist on the table, but missed it and just hit the air. He walked out of the bar, staggering quite a bit.

The two women looked at each other, shaking their heads.

"Wow, I guess I'll be avoiding this bar from now on when I have cabin fever," said Lani.

"Yeah, Hana is not a good place to be when you have cabin fever," replied Alana. "There are not many choices. Although, I guess you could always go to your friends' houses. You are always welcome at my place, for example."

"Thanks. The same goes for you. I didn't know Billy is out of town."

"The hotel sent him to Kahului. He has to take some electrician class. He can do a lot of electrical stuff at the hotel, but for some things you need a special certification."

The bartender came over and apologized.

"I'm sorry that you had to put up with that guy. He acts as if he owns the place after drinking too much, and that happens quite a bit," he said. "Drinks are on the house." He looked at Alana. "What can I get you, Alana?"

She looked at Lani. "What are you having?"

"A Hana Hotel Mai Tai," she replied.

"I'll have the same," answered Alana. "I can use one right now."

The barkeeper came up with her Mai Tai.

"Thank you," said Alana to the barkeeper.

Lani remembered something. She had brought the newspaper article to show Alana.

"I forgot to tell you about this. I was helping Phillip at Maui Exotics unwrap orchids from a nursery in Honolulu, and one of them was wrapped in this piece of newspaper." She pointed at the woman in the photo. "Do you think this could be Luana?"

Alana stared at the newspaper article. "I really can't tell. But that painting in the background certainly is her. You've seen that, haven't you? Boy, why would anyone but Luana have that…"

Lani nodded.

"I am flying to Honolulu tomorrow. I really have to go and see if it's her. Did I tell you that Pineapple Peter thinks he might have seen her in Honolulu years ago too?"
Alana was excited to hear that.

"Please let me know what you find out." She looked at Lani for a while and said: "I'm actually glad that you came and this whole story is being warmed up again. People in town, who haven't been speaking for thirty years, are starting to talk to each other again. And I'm glad to know you."

"Same here," replied Lani with a smile.
They chatted for a while about this and that. When it was time to go home and Lani got up, she felt the alcohol in the Mai Tai and wondered if she should still be driving. Oh, well, it was only one, she thought to herself. I should be okay.

Alana lived right around the corner in walking distance from Hana Hotel, but Lani insisted on driving her home. She dropped Alana off, turned around and drove past the Hana Hotel, the general store and the gas station. She was driving very slowly with the windows open, because it was such a balmy night and she was a bit insecure about driving in the dark here by herself. She slowed down even more when she saw a few pedestrians walking past the gas station. It was some older locals who had been drinking at the Henderson Ranch Restaurant. They recognized Lani and one of them yelled:

"Oh look, there's the half breed," and they all started laughing.
Lani's blood pressure shot up immediately. She was unbelievably upset. She had never been insulted like that in her entire life. She looked in her rear view mirror. She didn't see the men anymore, so she stopped in one of the entrances of Henderson Ranch on the right side of the road. She just sat there, breathing in and out to calm herself down. Maybe it's time to leave Hana, she thought to herself. But then she tried to think of all the kind and loving people she had met here, sighed a deep sigh and continued her drive to Koki Beach House. There will always be haters, she thought and took a left into the driveway.
The lights in the guesthouse were off.

Chapter 53

The next morning, Lani almost overslept. She quickly jumped out of bed, ran over to the coffee maker and made some strong coffee. She ran upstairs to get ready for her trip. After taking a shower, she came back downstairs with her toilet kit and packed it into her carry-on, along with a change of clothes for tonight and tomorrow.

She poured herself a coffee and stuck a piece of toast in the toaster. She quickly made a peanut butter and jelly toast, ate some fruit and soon she was on her way.

Max's truck was gone.

The Hana airport was tiny. It was about three miles outside of Hana. It was basically just a small one-room building with one counter, a waiting area and a single asphalt runway with low green shrubs on both sides and the ocean in the background. The far side of the runway looked like it ended in the water. The building was surrounded by a low stone wall with some pieces of white picket fence. She parked her car in a small parking lot and checked in at the counter and still had some time to sit down. She loved flying, so she was excited about a trip in a small propellor plane and couldn't wait to see Maui from above. There were only two other passengers besides her.

The plane was a small propeller Maui Airlines aircraft. When Lani boarded the plane, she found out what it meant when they advertised that every seat was a window seat. There were only nine seats in total on the plane and one on each side per row. Her seat was in the front of the plane. She sat down and buckled up, while the female captain made her announcement:

"Good morning, ladies and gentlemen. We welcome you on board the 208EX Cessna Grand Caravan aircraft Maui N895 MA. We will be cruising in an average height of 4,000 – 5,000 ft. We will be making a brief stop in Kahului to let some additional passengers get on the plane and then continue our flight to Honolulu International Airport with a slightly higher altitude. Please keep your seatbelts fastened for the entire duration of our twenty-minute flight for your safety. Due to the short duration of the flight, we will not be serving beverages or snacks at this time. Now please sit back and we hope you enjoy Maui's beautiful coastline from the air."

Hawaiian music started playing through the loudspeakers, as the plane quickly accelerated and took off. Lani felt like in a rollercoaster, because she could feel every tiny movement of the plane. The views were stunning. They flew along the cliffs and green valleys at the coastline and above the Road to Hana with very detailed views of some things you couldn't see from the road. She saw Black Sand Beach and the black lava cliffs in Waianapanapa State Park, another place on her list that she hadn't had a chance to visit yet. She saw the Hana Highway from above. It looked like a snake, twisting and turning along the coast, but the road wasn't very visible most of the time, because it was covered by the big African Tulip Trees and other rainforest plants from above. The ocean was light to dark blue and Lani could still see the white foamy tips of the waves at the shoreline. Lani could see some waterfalls that you couldn't see from the road. She also saw the tip of majestic Haleakala sticking out of the clouds. Soon the plane was already landing in Kahului.

"Ladies and gentlemen, welcome to Kahului. We will be stopping here for about twenty minutes and then continue our flight to Honolulu. Please remain seated," said the pilot through the intercom system.

Two more people boarded the plane and the flight could continue. The plane flew over the West Maui Mountains and Molokai – another destination she would love to visit. Soon the plane was flying over South-East Oahu and the passengers could see Diamond Head from the air.

Chapter 54

A few minutes later, the plane landed at Honolulu International
Airport. Lani and the other passengers disembarked the plane and
entered the arrival terminal. Just like in Maui, the airport had an almost
open-air feeling and was very tropical. She had to go to baggage claim
to wait for her carry-on, because the plane was too small for big
overhead bins and all bags had to be checked. Then she went and got her
small rental car and checked the time on her phone. It was 2:30.

She googled the address of Blue Tropics Nursery in Palolo Valley –
it was half an hour to drive out there, so she still had plenty of time until
they closed. She could grab something to eat on the way. She had to
drive straight past Waikiki on Route I-H 1 E, but got a little distracted
when she saw signs to Waikiki Beach and thought she'd make a little
detour and have lunch in Waikiki… Traffic was busy and she got stuck
in stop and go traffic with tourists driving slowly, dropping people off or
just stopping to take pictures in the middle of the road, so that she
almost regretted her decision, but it was still worth seeing the hustle and
bustle of Waikiki Beach on Kalakaua Avenue. One skyscraper stood
next to the other, they reached almost down to the ocean with a narrow
strip of beach, Waikiki Beach. There were upscale designer shops,
jewelry stores, bars and restaurants, tourist shops and the sidewalks were
full of tourists, walking up and down, taking pictures with their cameras
and shopping.
When she saw a little food truck, she stopped on the side of the road
and grabbed a bite to eat. She noticed a sign on a lamppost that
advertised for a Jazz Combo that was playing in various locations in
Honolulu in the next few days. It was a combo called "Mandy sings the
Mamba" and they were obviously playing at Jay's Hawaii Bar tonight.
Lani briefly felt a twitch in her heart, but she thought to herself: "Maybe
I should go and check out if that's THE Mandy…" She was curious.
And she had heard a lot about Jay's Hawaii Bar, which would be a fun
place to have dinner.

She got back into her car, took a left in front of Diamond Head and was now headed to the outskirts of Honolulu and Palolo Valley where Blue Tropics Orchids was located.

Lani parked her car on a dirt patch where other cars were parked and walked up to the gigantic greenhouses. She looked for a sign and quickly found one that said: "Entrance" and another one that said: "Yes, We are Open".

She walked into the greenhouse and immediately started breaking out in a sweat.

The first room was a sales and showroom. A young man was sitting in a little office in the back. Lani walked up to him, introduced herself and showed him the newspaper article that she had brought with her.

"Aloha, I'm Lani from Hana. I'm looking for this woman."
The young man said "Aloha" and looked at the newspaper article.

"Yeah, that's Ana and Patrick and all of the people who work here." He pointed at one of the people in the photo. "That's me… Unfortunately, Ana and Patrick are not here right now. They're both at the Santa Barbara International Orchid Show for the entire week."

Lani was very disappointed. She hadn't even thought about the possibility of the woman in the photo not being there. She wondered if Luana had shortened her name to Ana. She looked around and spotted the painting in the newspaper article on the back wall of the office.

"What's your name? Alex?" she said, looking at his nametag. "Would you mind if I took a look at that painting?" she asked and first pointed at the wall, then at the newspaper. He nodded and she stepped up to the painting.

Lani examined the painting. It was a beautiful small 16 x 16 inch portrait of Luana. It was the painting that Paul Kent had given Luana when they last saw each other, which of course Lani didn't know. Of course, as usual, it had a striking resemblance with Lani.

Alex watched her and his jaw dropped, he also saw the similarity between Lani and the girl in the painting.

"Wow, you look exactly like…" But he stopped talking.

He was uncomfortable. What if this lady wanted something or pretended to be a relative… He was responsible for the whole place while his bosses were away and would rather not discuss anything with this stranger. He became quiet and only gave her one-syllable answers. He'd rather call his bosses when she was gone and ask them what to do.

"Yes, an amazing resemblance," Lani replied. "When are they coming back from Santa Barbara?"

"Next Thursday," Alex answered. "I can give you their cell phone number, if you'd like."

He gave her a business card, which had both Patrick's and Ana's phone mobile number on it. She thanked him and asked:

"While I'm here, would you mind if I took a look at the nursery? I'm actually an avid orchid collector myself and have my own little nursery in the Hudson Valley in New York. Here's my business card, just in case Ana wants to get in touch with me."

"Of course. I'm open another half hour, but I can stay longer if you need a while."

"Thank you." replied Lani and headed into the first one of several gigantic greenhouses.

Even though she worked in the nursery business herself, she had never seen such a big nursery, filled EXCLUSIVELY with orchids. It was a dream come true for her. There were entire rows of one single species, and all were blooming at the same time. It was beautiful. She wished she had about two more days to look at all of the orchids and that she could take some back with her.

Lani finally tore herself away from the orchids and drove back to Waikiki Beach, where she had booked a middle class hotel right on the beach. She parked the car, checked in, brought her things up and changed. She didn't have time to enjoy her nice hotel room with a view, but she stood on her balcony for a few minutes, looking down at Waikiki at night. The view was absolutely stunning and she became a bit blue, because it would have been twice as nice with Max. She tried to forget about him for now, grabbed her purse and left her room to take the elevator down and dive into the nightlife of Waikiki.

Chapter 55

Lani walked down the main drag and arrived in front of Jay's Hawaii Bar that was totally packed, but she made her way thought the crowd and was able to grab a single seat at the packed bar next to a young surfer dude with blonde dreadlocks. It was a great place for „people watching". The median age was 25, lots of people still had their bathing suits on and seemed to be hanging out and having a few beers after a day of surfing. The combo was currently playing on the outside patio. It was indeed "The" Mandy. Lani was amazed about what a great singing voice she had despite her squeaky Minnie Mouse voice when she talked, and a little twinge of jealousy went through her heart again. The combo created a very tropical atmosphere - they were playing Island Music, and not really Jazz. Besides singing, Mandy was playing the ukulele.

After Lani had ordered a beer and the catch of the day and had almost finished eating her meal and the surfer dude and she had started a conversation, the band finished their song and announced that they were taking a fifteen-minute break. Mandy and the three musicians all walked into the bar area, where Mandy walked up to the blonde surfer dude, nestled up against him and took a sip of his drink. She immediately recognized Lani, her eyes got wide & she said in a loud voice to drown out all of the other voices:

„Wow, what brings you here Alani?"

„It's Lani. Hi, Mandy!"

Mandy didn't even wait for an answer.

„Is Max here too?"

„No, I'm here on business, by myself."

Mandy looked at her boyfriend and introduced him. „Oh, Lani, this is my boyfriend Jack."

They both nodded. „We've already met," said Jack. Jack recognized a friend in the other corner of the bar and who was just leaving and excused himself. „Excuse me, ladies, I'll be right back. I just want to say hi to an old friend over there. He seems to be leaving."

Mandy took the opportunity that she was alone with Lani and said:

„Listen, I saw how upset you were the other day at your house and just wanted to apologize for coming over without calling. There is nothing going on between Max and me. Please don't even mention Max to Jack, he's really jealous. I just didn't know where else to go the other day. Hana doesn't really have a lot of hotels and I can't afford the Hana Hotel… I really think Max likes you…"
Lani nodded. "Thanks."

Maybe Mandy wasn't so bad after all. And maybe Max did really love her. Her heart skipped a beat. She missed him.

****

The next morning, the weather was quite overcast, but the sun came out quickly while Lani was heaving breakfast on the beautiful terrace of the hotel overlooking Waikiki Beach. Her flight back to Maui was at 1 pm, so she had about four hours until she had to be at the airport, and decided to drive to Chinaman's Hat. Chinaman's Hat had always been one of the famous landmarks of Oahu that she had wanted to see. If she didn't make too many stops and stay too long, she'd be back at the airport on time. She checked out of the hotel, put her carry-on case into the trunk of her car and departed.

She called Anne quickly to make sure everything in the nursery was okay and that the broken irrigation pipe had been taken care of. Anne, with Bill's assistance, was doing a great job and everything was fine. Anne told Lani some news that Lani was quite pleased about:
"Bill and I went out for dinner the other night, Lani. It was quite nice. I might have to say that I have a crush on him after working so closely with him…"

The drive from Waikiki to Chinaman's Hat was beautiful. Lani drove up Kamahameha Highway, the scenery switched from from mountain ridges and beautiful valleys on both sides to scenic ocean views and bays. The weather kept changing from very cloudy to sunny. After a 40 minute drive, Lani saw Chinaman's Hat right in front of her. In back of her were the East Oahu Mountains. She parked in Kualoa Beach Park, a big grassy park in front of Chinaman's Hat. On the edge of the park was a shave ice stand, which she couldn't resist, even though she had eaten quite a big breakfast not too long ago. While she enjoyed her shave ice, she checked her travel guide and then went for a quick swim in the ocean. When it was finally time to head back, she got back in the car and drove straight through to the airport, enjoying the views of the beautiful mountain ridges again.

As soon as the plane took off, she fell asleep and slept almost the entire flight back. She just woke up briefly for the stop in Kahului and then fell asleep again. When the plane landed, she was mad at herself for missing all of the beautiful views on the way back in the plane. It was already early evening when she landed in Hana. It felt like coming home when she drove through town, continued to Koki Beach and then took a left into the driveway of Koki Beach House.

Chapter 56

It was early evening and Max's truck was in the driveway. One of the surfboards was gone, a sure sign he was down at the beach. Lani really wanted to see him and some time in the cool saltwater would feel nice after sitting in a car and a plane the entire day, so she quickly took her things inside, changed into a bathing suit, grabbed her beachbag and a cold bottle of water. Outside, she tucked the second surfboard under her arm and walked down to Hamoa Beach.

Max was far out in the ocean, hanging out on his surfboard, waiting for the next perfect wave. The ocean was a bit rougher today, so she was a bit nervous when she pushed her surfboard into the water, past the first small wavebreak, laid down on it and started paddling out toward Max. She quickly arrived next to Max, who was surprised and obviously very pleased to see her.

She waved at him, turned her surfboard around and was a bit shocked about how far out she was. These were "real" waves, not the waves she had surfed on for the first time with Max, and not the calm water that she had tried to surf in when she went by herself…

Max made a sign and pointed out toward the ocean. A perfect wave was coming. They both started paddling. Max was soon riding the wave, skilled and experienced. Lani, however, didn't paddle fast enough and was basically swallowed by the wave. She spun around in all directions and felt like she was in a washing machine. This time she couldn't feel the sand under her feet. The water was deep, dark and very salty. She felt the surfboard tugging at her ankle and thought for a second it would probably hit her head. She came up coughing, her nose full of water, but the next wave was already there and washed over her as well. Again, she was spun around. As soon as she came up the next time, she immediately tried to swim away from the next wave that she knew was coming. Her eyes, nose and mouth were full of salty water. Max had seen what was happening and came swimming up quickly. He helped pull the surfboard closer and pushed Lani on top of it, where she got a short break and was able to wipe the water out of her eyes. The next wave was coming, but the water was shallow enough now and this one was gentler. She paddled as fast as she could, but didn't try to get up anymore. She was too exhausted. She just wanted to get out of the water and take a break on land. Max followed her, swimming, and arrived on the beach just a few seconds after Lani. Max kneeled down next to Lani, who was sitting on her surfboard right where the foamy water hit the sand, trying to calm herself down.

"Are you okay, Lani?" Max was really worried.

"I'm fine, just embarrassed…"

"That's no reason to be embarrassed. Do you know how many times that's happened to me?" Max asked. "And those waves out there are a bit too big for a beginner today."
She just sat there, breathing hard.

"You know what they say about falling off of a horse, don't you? Do you want to try again?"

Lani didn't want to try again. Right now, she just wanted to lie on the beach and have Max wrap his strong tanned arms around her. And he did. They just lay there, in the shoreline, kissing each other, while the setting sun created a beautiful scene, dipped in all shades of red.

It was almost dark when they finally walked home. Nothing needed to be said. They were content just walking next to each other, their surfboards under their arms. The last birds of the day were still singing and the cicadas were making their loud buzzing sound. Max picked a plumeria from one of the trees on the side of the road and handed it to Lani with a smile. She smiled back at him and stuck it behind her ear.

They set their surfboards down against the side of the guesthouse and Max automatically walked inside with her.
Lani said: "I was just going to warm up some leftovers. Is that okay with you?"
He nodded. "Sounds good."
They walked into the kitchen, where Lani started warming up the leftover meat sauce in a frying pan. She put a bottle of wine and two glasses on the counter and filled both of them. She continued stirring the

meat sauce, while she remembered the big manila envelope with the photos that was standing upright on the counter leaning against the tile.

"You're not going to believe what I found the other day while I was cleaning up all the painting supplies upstairs. It must have fallen out from in between the paintings. Take a look, my hands might have sauce on them."

He took the envelope, looked inside and pulled out the photos.

"Wow. That's incredible," Max was very impressed. He looked through the photos.

"The unbelievable thing is that you seriously look exactly like her. She was certainly gorgeous. And he was a great photographer."
He looked at a photo of Paul Kent.

"It's hard to believe that you're his daughter with your Polynesian features. You certainly look more like your mother," he said holding the photo of Paul Kent up next to Lani's face. "Oh, wait, your eyes look like his…"

Max put the photos back into the envelope and just sat there with his glass of wine and watched her. He couldn't just sit there though, got up and walked to the other side of the counter, next to Lani. She was like a magnet to him.

"Can I help with anything?"

"Yes, you could just warm up the spaghetti. Just put it in a bowl, sprinkle them with some water and put them in the microwave. And could you also grate some new Parmesan cheese? I could only find a big piece at the store."
She got a big piece of Parmesan out of the fridge and handed him the grater.

They worked hand in hand and made quite a good team.

Soon, they were sitting on the deck, both with a plate of spaghetti and meat sauce leftovers in front of them, their wine glasses, a bottle of water and some tealights in between them. It was quite a romantic atmosphere and there was quite a lot of warmth between them as they flirted and joked around.

"How was Oahu?" asked Max.

"I love it, what a different pace than Maui, but the woman who I think might be my mother wasn't there. She was at an orchid show in California, so now I won't get a chance to see if it's her for a while…"

"You never know. Maybe you'll be back faster than you think," replied Max, full of hope.

They just sat there for a while silently and listened to the ocean pound against the rocks.

"I saw Mandy perform at Jay's Hawaii Bar…"

"What?" he perked his ears, a bit nervous. "That's hilarious. Was it a coincidence?"

"No, I saw a poster that she was singing there and just decided to go and check it out… I talked to her. She told me that there's nothing going on between the two of you… She was actually quite nice."

She looked at him across the table. He put his hands on hers and pulled her closer for a gentle kiss. They both took their wine glasses, got up and stood at the railing, arm in arm, looking into each other's eyes, enjoying each other's company. They gently started kissing each other and the moon disappeared between the clouds…

Chapter 57

Max was off for the next three days, so the next morning, they were able to sleep the Sleep of the Innocent and both got some well-needed rest. They spent a beautiful day at the beach and in the evening they wanted to go and have dinner at Henderson Ranch Restaurant.

As they walked toward Max's truck, they both looked up toward the street. A brand new Range Rover SUV with dark tinted windows was standing in the driveway. They walked up to the car to see if the passengers needed help or directions. The window rolled down and Lani recognized Joseph, the same man who had accosted her in the bar of Hana Hotel the other day, in the driver's seat. A slender beautiful blonde in a tight sundress revealing her curves and wearing giant designer sunglasses was sitting in the passenger seat.

Max asked: "Can we help you?"

"No, thank you. We're just interested in this property..." replied Joseph McAllen.

Lani became pale. "It's not for sale. Yet." she said with a firm voice.

"Oh, I heard the renovation is not going very well," replied Joseph.

"Who told you that?" asked Lani with a sharp voice.

"Come on, Lani, we have to go." said Max and turned toward the man. "Please leave and don't come here anymore. This is private property."

He put his arm around Lani's shoulders and pulled her around, back toward the cars.

The windows of the Range Rover were rolled up and the SUV departed.

Max turned to Lani. "Don't let that guy bother you. He shows up here from time to time and acts as if he owns the place. He is a nobody."

"Oh my gosh, I was at the bar of Hana Hotel the other night with Alana and he totally accosted us in a really creepy manner."

"Try to ignore him," said Max. He tried to act cool, but his blood was boiling as well...

The drive into Hana was beautiful, as usual. It was getting dark, but everything was still slightly lit in beautiful pale colors, the ocean looked unusually calm and eerie tonight and there were dark clouds on the horizon.

"It almost seems like the calm before a storm," said Max, also looking briefly out toward the ocean while he was driving. "Look at those clouds over there."

Lani nodded. The ocean and sky did look different than she had ever seen them before.

Max turned the radio on and searched for the weather channel.

The weather forecaster announced: "There is a strong thunderstorm and wind advisory in effect in Hana until 7 pm HST this evening, also a flash flood watch. We advise you to stay off of the Hana Highway and away from any waterfalls and other areas where flashflooding is possible until this advisory has been lifted."

Max looked at Lani. "Wow, we might get stuck at Henderson's, but I guess we can just play it by ear. Thunderstorms like that are pretty rare in Maui and it should be over quickly."

Lani nodded. She didn't mind. She was used to bad thunderstorms, and she found it quite romantic being stuck with Max somewhere, anywhere...

As they arrived at the Henderson Ranch Restaurant, they heard thunder in the distance, which seemed to be coming closer and closer. The lightning flashes seemed to be all around them, and soon it started pouring.

They had just started their meal, when Max received an emergency call from the fire department. A house had obviously been struck by lightning and someone had reported a fire. Everyone in the area who was on call was to come to the fire department immediately. Max put his phone back in his pocket and looked at Lani.

"I'm sorry, there's an emergency. I'm going to have to leave right now. The problem is that you won't have a ride home. As soon as I know how long I'll be, I'll call, okay?"

"Don't worry about me," said Lani with a smile. "You have to go. Maybe I can call Alana and she can give me a ride home."

Max rushed off and minutes later, Lani heard the sirens of a firetruck driving by. She felt proud of Max, but was also worried. She had never thought about how dangerous his job was…

Lani called Alana. Billy, who worked with Max at the fire department, had been called as well, so Alana was very happy to come and pick Lani up and drive her home. She was there within ten minutes. As they drove past Koki Beach and down Haneoo Road, Lani's heart started beating uncontrollably. They could see the flashing lights of the firetrucks and they recognized that the house on fire was Koki Beach House! It looked like the fire had been in the bedroom facing the guesthouse, because that's where firefighters were currently working, but it looked like everything was already under control.

Lani got out of the car and discovered Max in his firefighter uniform, working. He discovered Lani and Alana and walked over to them. He took Lani in his arms and said:

"I'm so sorry, Lani."

"Oh my gosh, do you have any idea what happened? Was the house hit by lightning?"

"Yes, it looks like it. The lightning possibly caused a fire on the side, but something inside exacerbated the fire, possibly the paint thinners, and it spread. We had it contained pretty quickly though, so it didn't cause very much damage besides in the upper bedroom. We did have to add some class A foam, because of the possible chemicals."

Lani was still in shock and sat down on one of the steps leading to the breezeway.

While all of Max's coworkers were packing up the firetruck and getting ready to depart, Max sat down next to Lani and held her. Alana joined them and gave Lani a hug from the other side.

"Are you okay, Lani?"

"Not really. But I guess it could have been worse."

"Please let me know if you need anything tomorrow. Both Billy and I are off and we can come over and help. Max, doesn't the fire department own that HEPA vacuum that we can use to vacuum the soot particles?"

"Yes, we do. I think we can open all of the windows. It looks like the rain is over for now. You can sleep at my place tonight, Lani. We also still have the big fans from the company in Kahului. We can put them into the bedroom and that will start drying out the water. But we worked very cautiously and the damage should be minimal."

Max got up. He had to ride back to the fire department with his colleagues to get changed, and his car was still there too.

"I'll be right back, Lani," he said to Lani, who still seemed in shock and just nodded, so he took Alana aside and asked: "Would you mind sticking around a little until I'm back? I'm a little worried about Lani. This is a bit much for her…"

Alana nodded. She was glad to help. The house was quite a project to have to deal with on your own and this fire was not what she needed on top of everything else. Alana really wanted Lani to be able to come back and was going to support her with whatever she needed. She sat down next to Lani and said in an upbeat manner:

"Come on, love, let's go and sit on the back deck and I'll make you a nice cup of tea for your nerves. Sometimes things look a little hopeless, but you will get back on your feet in no time. You're a fighter! And believe me, this house is still worth it, even if you think it isn't right now."

Lani looked up and smiled at Alana. "Thanks, Alana, you're so sweet. I really appreciate your and Billy's help – and Max's."

They walked to the back deck and Alana went inside to make a cup of tea.

Max was back soon with Billy who would ride home with Alana. He and Billy had a beer while they talked about their plans to clean up the areas tomorrow that had been damaged by smoke and fire. Billy knew what he was talking about. He had done fire and smoke cleanup before.

"There should be as much airflow in the house as possible. So, if you're sensitive," he said to Lani, "you should sleep at Max's place and keep your bedroom door closed and open up everything else. And turn all the fans on. I will come over first thing in the morning to check if I can do the work or if we have to hire a company with more equipment. It's no rush, since you're leaving on Sunday, correct?" he asked Lani.

"Yes," replied Lani and her eyes filled up with some more tears.

"Do you think we have to inform the insurance company?" asked Max.

"Probably," replied Billy, "but I'm afraid, if those old chemicals were still up there, they might not pay."

Lani felt even worse. It was her fault. She was the one who had been in a rush the other day when Aaron and William had come over and she hadn't taken the time to take the box with the chemicals out of the house. She had even broken one of the bottles and left all the soiled papertowels up there...

"I guess we can always try," said Max. He looked at Lani and said: "I'll call the insurance company on Monday, don't worry about it. And even if they don't pay, the damage is not so bad that it will make you lose the house..."

Lani nodded thankfully, but she wasn't so sure about that. My last 36 hours in Hana are going to be quite sad, she thought to herself. She was very quiet the rest of the evening and on the verge of giving up. Alana and Billy left early to let her and Max get some rest.

They sat on the deck for another while, but then walked over to the guesthouse and went to bed very early. Lani fell asleep and slept a long and dreamless sleep, while Max lay next to her, watching her sleep and not able to fall sleep himself. He didn't want her to leave...

Chapter 58

The next day, the weather was back to beautiful with a slight chance of showers, as usual. Keanu and Billy came over to help Max with some first post fire clean up work. There was a lot to do, but everyone was upbeat and ready to take on the challenges.

Everyone except Lani. She had a hard time snapping out of the feeling of being overwhelmed and that she couldn't handle all this. Her departure tomorrow evening felt like a big weight on her shoulders. Max had given her the job of taking everything out of the upper bedroom that she thought was worth keeping, and so she was not only finally taking the old painting supplies, that hadn't been affected by the fire, down to the garage, but she was also going through everything else in the bedroom and putting things worth keeping into the other bedroom on the opposite side of the house. Alana had also come and was helping her, while she tried to cheer her up, but she didn't have much luck.

Lani also worked on cleaning other parts of the house and doing laundry, so that she could start packing in the evening.

They all had a nice lunch on the deck and then everyone had to leave and Max and Lani were alone. Max walked up to Lani who was sitting on the deck, staring out at the ocean, and said: "Come on, Lani! Cheer up! You're in paradise! How about going surfing to take your mind off of the house?"

Lani thought that was a good idea, forced herself to a smile and nodded. "Yeah, that's a good idea. Let's go."
While they walked to the beach, she said:
"I'm sorry that I'm so negative today. I'm just really having a hard time leaving…"
He put his arm around her, pulled her closer, gave her a kiss on the cheek and said:
"You'll be back."
"I hope so…"

They put their things onto the rocks in the back under the trees as usual and walked straight down to the water with their surfboards. Today, the surf Gods smiled down upon Lani and she was able to ride a few waves, which distracted her and got rid of the lump in her throat, at least for a while. The water, the sun, beautiful Hamoa Beach and Max made her forget all of her troubles and breathe clearly. After they were done surfing, they just laid in the shade and looked up into the crowns of the palm trees and held each other. As the sun was getting ready to go down, they packed up and walked back slowly to Koki Beach House.

"Since we couldn't really enjoy our dinner at Henderson's last night, what do you think about going back today?" asked Max. She didn't mind the distraction and agreed.

She walked up to her bathroom to take a shower and change, while Max went over to the guesthouse to get some fresh clothes. After she was done getting ready and on her way downstairs, she heard the sound of tires driving onto the gravel driveway. Lani looked out of the office window in the front and saw at least ten to fifteen cars, parking in the driveway and in the street. Max was outside, waiting for them.

Lani went to the front door, opened it and walked outside.

Her grandfather, even her grandmother with her walker, and at least twenty other people were getting out of their cars: A few carpenters, a builder, a painter, of course Max's friends Keanu and Billy with Alana, some of Max's firefighter coworkers and some other helpful handy people. It was Lani's grandparents and the people of Hana, who had buried the feud between each other and had been united again. Max stepped next to Lani.

Kumu walked up to Lani and made an announcement:

"I was a gosh darn fool," he said. "It doesn't matter if my grandchild is from a brown man, a black man or a white man. We all have the same colored blood. Malani was a smart woman. She didn't only give you this house because you deserve it, but also to bring this town back together. We have ended this silly feud and we all want to help you return and fix up this house Malani gave you. We will all work together. We can do it. And I hope you can forgive me one day."

Between the paintings and photos she had found, the exhibit Aaron wanted to have, selling her nursery or shares of it and the help of the people of Hana, Lani suddenly felt confident that she would be able to start with the renovations. It would be risky and expensive, but it would be worth it. Some friends had already shown her today how much you can get done when you work hand in hand.

Lani had to fly back to the Hudson Valley on Sunday to find a long-term solution for her nursery and file the paperwork to bring the Bassets. But she knew she'd return, and soon.

She looked at Max. Max looked at her. They fell into each other's arms and, since the people of Hana had all brought something to eat and drink, a spontaneous party began on the back deck of Koki Beach House. Lani looked at Max and the partygoers and then out at the beautiful Pacific Ocean. And she knew she was Home.

...to be continued...